ALPHA MAIL

Cover Designer
Regina Wamba, Mae I Design
www.maeidesign.com

Cover Photographer
Sara Eirew
www.saraeirew.com

Editor
Lisa Hollett, Silently Correcting Your Grammar

Copy Editor
Taylor Bellitto

Interior Design and Formatting
Christine Borgford, Type A Formatting
www.typeAformatting.com

ALPHA MAIL

Brenda Rothert

ONE

#likeaboss

THIRTY-SEVEN EXTREMELY HOT men are looking at me, each one listening to my every word. Most twenty-eight-year-old women would be loving it, but me? I'm frustrated as hell right now.

"How much clearer can I be, you guys? No dick pics. Ever. It doesn't matter if it's *your* dick or not, we don't transmit lewd images at Alpha Mail."

A blond guy in the front row, whose name I can't remember, frowns at me. "But we're supposed to keep the customer happy . . ."

"Women can live full and thrilling lives without ever getting a dick pic," I say, an edge of frustration in my tone.

"But on the platinum plan, we can get as dirty as the customer wants."

Who *is* this guy? Does he not realize he's talking to the owner of the company? I give him a tight smile.

"Our procedure manual is very clear that the platinum plan includes dirty texts and phone sex. No photos."

"What if the customer sends photos first? What if they *ask* for dick pics?"

I take a calming breath before responding. "It's still a no. You know how to handle requests that are against our rules."

He nods, and I think it's finally sinking in. But then he furrows his brow. "But what if it's . . . just the tip?"

There's a snicker from the back row.

"Did you seriously just ask that?" I shake my head.

He shrugs, his cheeks reddening. "I mean . . . what if it's only part of . . . you know?"

I hold up a hand to emphasize the point I'm about to make. "No photos. None. No photos of dicks, dick tips, faces, chests, balls, or even kittens."

My company's marketing guru and close friend, Gretchen, must sense my irritation, because she steps in.

"Tyler, we're going to have you repeat the training on this."

I glance down at my notes and see that my next point is going to take a while, so I dismiss everyone for a fifteen-minute break. The guys all head straight for the lounge, which is always stocked with coffee, doughnuts, sandwiches, fruit, and other snacks and drinks. I found out early on that the key to keeping a twenty-to-fortysomething male workforce happy is plentiful food and drinks.

When I'm left alone in the conference room, my mind starts racing with nervous anticipation. There are so many things I want to perfect about Alpha Mail before the tour we're doing in a few days for investors.

Even though I have a team that monitors all the communications between our team of alphas and clients, it would only take one mistake to give the whole company a black eye. One man who takes things too far or says something offensive, and we'd have a PR nightmare on our hands. I have a team for that too, but you know what they say about an ounce of prevention.

I need this investor meeting to go well. My company is thriving and growing at an unexpectedly fast rate, and this will help us build it strategically. I never imagined the idea I hatched over drinks with my best friend Carmen two years ago would grow into what it has.

"I've had enough of alphas," I grumbled to her that night after yet another relationship had ended. "They're too possessive and temperamental."

"Not all alphas are as extreme as Tony," Carmen had said, rolling her eyes as she referenced the man I'd just broken up with. "Taking you into a bar bathroom for a spanking because you made eye contact with another man isn't normal."

We'd laughed and drunk and laughed some more as we both lamented dates and relationships from men who'd said things like, *"This pussy belongs to me, kitten,"* and *"Who dis dick belong to, baby girl?"*

Alphas are often more irritating and amusing than hot, we'd agreed that night. I'd told Carmen I liked the racy texts and sexy goodnight phone calls from my alpha boyfriends, but not the part where I had to spend nearly all my free time with them and deal with their constant suspicions and jealousies.

Someone needed to start a business where women could subscribe to get texts and phone calls from sexy, brooding alpha types without the bullshit relationship part, I'd told Carmen over our second pitcher of margaritas.

Alpha Mail had been born, my initial business plan written on a napkin at the bar that night as sort of a joke. But when I delved further into the idea after my hangover passed, there was nothing funny about it.

It was solid, fresh, and utterly perfect for the modern woman who's over the dating scene. Keep that heart-racing thrill of getting sexy, sometimes sweet messages from a hot man, and *also* keep your time free for work, school, or friends.

I'd hoped a hundred women would sign up when my initial

marketing campaign started. Instead, 486 had signed up in the first week.

"Sienna?" Gretchen passes me a bottle of water, bringing me back to the present.

"Hmm?" I shake my head and smile at her. "Oh, thanks."

"I can handle this next part if you need me to. I know you have financials to go through."

A corner of my mouth quirks up in a smile. "Did you ever think you'd use your MBA to discuss when to use the word *cock* and when to use *dick* when texting clients of the company you work for?"

Gretchen smiles back and shrugs. "It's a lot more interesting than my last job. I had to write marketing copy for nursing homes there."

"That sounds kinda depressing."

"Sometimes. And also ridiculous. My boss insisted we make the places sound like vacation resorts. Fun, adventurous, and sexy!" She rolls her eyes as she imitates her former boss's excitement.

"Sexy?" I arch my brows skeptically. "A *nursing home?*"

She nods soberly. "You saved me from the campaign they were making me head up called *The Old and the Beautiful.*"

"Shut up."

"Not even kidding."

Our male workforce comes trickling back into the room. Dan, an employee who asked me out recently, grins and winks in my direction as he sits down in the front row.

I sigh inwardly. I'd never, ever date an employee. That policy saved me from having to openly reject Dan, but he's still trying to convince me we could be involved on the side.

No way. I don't have the time or the interest. I spend at least twelve hours a day at the office—often more. And my off time is spent with Carmen and her six-year-old son, Jack. They moved in with me last year when Carmen had to quit her job to take care of Jack full time after he was diagnosed with Batten disease.

There are no easy days for Carmen, who is a single mom. My long workdays are nothing compared to what she goes through. If I can get the investment money I need for Alpha Mail, it will allow me to use some of my own money to hire home nurses to help. I dream of it every time I walk in my front door and see Carmen asleep on my couch, the dark circles beneath her eyes ever-present now.

"I've got this," I tell Gretchen. "But thanks. If you could maybe work on our investor packets for the meeting Friday?"

"Absolutely." She gives me a mock salute.

As Gretchen walks out of the room, I look out over the sea of muscles in front of me. When I was younger, I would have been hot and bothered by all this testosterone. Now I just see my employees—men who can be coached into the best alphas out there, helping build my company into a powerhouse.

"All right." I clear my throat and click to the next page of my PowerPoint presentation. "We're going to run through when it's best to use and not use certain words—specifically fuck, cock, and dick."

There's a hum of amused laughter from my audience.

"I know." I give them a quick smile. "But believe it or not, if we use these words sparingly in our client communications, it really ups their impact. So, let's start with—" I bring up the first slide "—fuck."

Let's start with fuck. My mind registers a joke in there somewhere, but I move on, focusing on my presentation. This is my last shot to strengthen our brand before the investor demo.

I just hope it will be enough. It has to. Carmen and Jack are counting on me.

ANDREW BENSON, A reporter for the *Chicago Sun*, is waiting
in a chair outside my office when I approach, moving as quickly
as I can in heels.

"Sorry." I smile at him. "My meeting ran over by a few minutes."

He grins back, brushing dark hair away from his eyes. "No
problem. I walked past the room as you were speaking. That sounded like . . . an *interesting* meeting."

"Yeah." I laugh lightly. "As you can imagine, our employees
have to be comfortable talking about things that aren't usually part
of an office environment."

He nods and arches his brows. "Ready for the interview?"

"Ready. Thanks for waiting. And thanks for the call. This is
going to be great exposure for Alpha Mail."

"I'm sure the story will get lots of reads. Our photographer
will be coming by in about an hour to get a photo of you to go
with the story."

I run a hand over my red hair, which is down around my
shoulders today. I'm wearing a black pencil skirt and a green blouse.
With a little lipstick and mascara, I can be photo-ready.

"Perfect."

"Ms. Mills, I have Conference Room One ready for you." My
assistant, Jane, gives me a confident smile.

She does an amazing job as my assistant. If I can get the investment I need to grow the business, I'm planning to promote
her into a role more suited for her talents. It'll mean training a
new assistant, but that's okay. I believe in rewarding hard work.

Andrew follows me into our makeshift conference room. It
has two tables pushed together that are surrounded by mismatched

chairs. I've focused my resources on building my base of employees, and things like office furniture have been neglected. Another area I plan to address if I can attract investors.

"So, want to start out by telling me where you got the idea for Alpha Mail?" he asks as he sits down.

He's almost handsome in a rumpled sort of way. With shaggy dark hair and glasses, I get a Clark Kent vibe from him. But he doesn't interest me enough to check for a wedding ring. I'm officially over men.

"I drew from my own experiences. I know there are women out there who like certain parts of dating, but other parts . . . not so much. So my goal was to help them cut through the whole process of dating and get only what they want."

"But the relationships they find through you . . . they aren't *real*, right?"

"They're real in their own way. They aren't exclusive, and they aren't physical, but when clients choose an alpha to communicate with, that's absolutely the only person they're hearing from."

Andrew quirks his lips into a smile. "What are the qualifications to be an alpha?"

"Alphas know what they want. They don't pussyfoot. They're domineering and often jealous and a bit controlling."

"And women are looking for that?"

Bless your heart, Clark Kent. You have no idea.

"Some women, sure. And I'm hoping they'll give Alpha Mail a try."

Jane brings in coffee, and we continue the interview for nearly an hour. When the photographer arrives, Andrew says he has everything he needs for his story. He shakes my hand and leaves, looking more than a little perplexed.

I wasn't really expecting him to get it. So many people think women are looking for a nice man who will open doors, kiss them goodnight, and not leave the toilet seat up. I'm sure a few of them *are* actually looking for that. But there are enough women dreaming of a dirty-talking alpha to grow my business into an empire.

And that's exactly what I plan to do with this pitch to investors.

TWO

TODAY'S THE DAY. I've done everything I can to prep for this investor meeting, but I'm still as nervous as I've ever been. I can sense a pimple beneath the surface of my skin on one cheek, which brings me right back to adolescence. Fucking nerves.

Gretchen's been by my side every step of the way, helping me answer every potential question and prepare for every potential pitfall. We've been awake all night, and we both just returned from our trips home to shower and dress for the meeting.

"How do I look?" I ask, passing her a giant paper cup of coffee I picked up on the way back.

She gives me a sheepish look. "Kinda awful."

"Awful?" My lips part with horror.

"You told me I should never lie to you."

"Well, shit." I set down my own cup of coffee and look down at my charcoal suit. "Should I change? I have a black dress in my office closet."

"No, your outfit's perfect."

"Then what is it?" My voice has a note of panic. "Is it the pimple? My hair?"

I reach back to undo the knot I put my long red hair back in, but Gretchen stops me with a shake of her head.

"No, Sienna. You look like you need to get laid and sleep for a good twelve hours."

I half gasp and half laugh at that. "True on both counts. But I can't do anything about either at the moment."

"We're ready." She gives me a confident nod. "You've earned this moment, so square your shoulders and go kick some ass."

I reach for her with a hug. "Thank you, G. I won't forget this."

"Me either," she says softly. "You listen to my ideas and make me feel valuable. That's . . . a really good feeling."

I pull back and smile at her. "Your ideas are great, and you *are* valuable to me."

Her eyes get a little misty, and I feel a lump in my throat. She clears her throat and says, "I'd totally give you millions of dollars if I were sitting at that table."

We're both laughing when Jane knocks on my office door.

"Come on in," I say.

Jane looks like a CEO herself today, wearing a sleek dark green dress. I can feel her nervous excitement. Everyone in our small company knows how important today's meeting is.

"Everyone's ready for you," she says. "I'm planning to bring in coffee again in about twenty minutes."

"Perfect."

My phone buzzes on my desk, and I glance down at it. The text on the screen from my older brother Coop makes me smile.

Coop: *Knock 'em dead today. And if any of them hits on you, call me and I'll kill 'em myself.*

He can be *a little bit* protective. And since our parents relocated to California a couple years ago, Coop is the only family I have nearby. I used to follow him and his friends around our suburban

Chicago neighborhood like a lost puppy, because I idolized my brother. I still do.

I text back a quick thanks and set my phone back on my desk, then head for the conference room. The racing of my heart intensifies as I get closer.

Outside the conference room, I pause and close my eyes. I *can't* blow this. If I don't get this money, it doesn't just mean old office furniture for the near future. Alpha Mail isn't about that for me.

I picture Jack's smile as I tickled him on the couch last weekend. His laugh is infectious. The kid melted my heart from the time he was born, but now that he's sick . . .

If I feel this helpless and desperate to help him, how does Carmen feel? She's his mother, and she'd lay down her life in a heartbeat to save her son, but unfortunately, she can't. Jack is going to get worse, and all we can do is love him, comfort him, and hire the best care money can buy.

That's where I come in. As I think about Jack, my heartbeat steadies. For him, I can do this. For him, I *will* do this.

I open the conference doors and walk into the room, which is full of men in dark suits. There are a few women sitting around the table too, one of them a former professor of mine from grad school. When I see several people standing against the wall, my confidence surges. I told the investors they could invite anyone else who might be interested, and it looks like they did.

"Thank you for joining us today." I take my spot at the head of the conference table. "I'm Sienna Mills."

Jane and Gretchen bring in extra chairs as I start my presentation. My graphic about the pitfalls of dating these days elicits several chuckles.

"I'm sure none of the men in this room has ever met a woman for a first date and asked her if she was up for a quickie in the bathroom before dinner arrived." That gets another laugh. "But it's happened to me."

I tell a couple more horror stories, one starring a woman who confessed to her date that she's usually only attracted to married men. That one happened to Carmen's friend Greg.

Both the men and women are nodding and smiling in agreement. Dating horror stories are universal. I'm about to move on to the presentation when my gaze stops for a second on a broad-shouldered man to my left, whose dark hair and eyes command attention. A flush of arousal distracts me as I stare openly for a second. I force myself to look at the man next to him instead, and . . .

Fuck me. Same guy? No, they're identical twins. They have to be Ben and Ian Durant, whose real estate investment success I'm familiar with. I invited them on a whim. Guess I should have checked to see how hot they were first. Those two could distract a postmenopausal nun.

It takes all my self-control to focus on my presentation, but I manage. I'm in the zone, hitting all my high points and getting nods every time I gauge reactions. I don't give my nerves a chance to surface.

Gretchen included the article Andrew wrote about Alpha Mail in the investor packet, and I notice a gray-haired investor reading it with an amused smile. Hopefully that's a good sign.

"I can talk about the business, but it doesn't compare to seeing it for yourself." I smile at the group and gesture toward the door. "So now we're going to let you have a look at the alphas at work."

I lead the group down the hallway, my heels clicking on the concrete floor as I walk. We make virtue of our office space being unfinished by calling it "modern." Brick interior walls, exposed ductwork, and raw concrete floors are design choices these days, and to save a few bucks, they became our style.

"We're going to watch Kell send texts to his clients."

I stop outside Kell's office, and the investors get their first look at him through the glass wall. I had all the offices here enclosed by glass walls rather than more private ones, so we could all have quiet to focus on our work, but we could still feel connected to each other. And to be honest, this way I know none of the alphas are taking photos or making videos that are against our policies. Having women beg for them has proved too tempting for some of my former employees.

"Kell was one of my first hires," I tell the group. "He's very popular with clients and is always fully booked."

That's an understatement. Between his blue eyes, handsome face, and smokin' hot body, Kell draws attention without saying a word. But when he *does* speak, panties drop. His Scottish accent is to die for. He's very good at what he does, which is why I chose him for the first demo.

"Morning," I say to him as I push open his office door and hold it open for the investors.

"Mornin'." Kell grins at the group and then turns back to the three computer monitors on his desk.

Investors cluster behind his desk to read the messages on his screens. Kell is in his usual work uniform of worn jeans and a white T-shirt, the sleeves tight around his biceps. He's totally in his element here, where he gets paid for his roguish ways. I smile as I scan the words on one of the monitors.

KELL: *Mornin, doll. Hope you slept well.*

LYDIAN: *Good morning! Mmm, would have slept better if you'd been next to me.*

KELL: *Yep, guarantee that. But I'd have kept you up late. You know I wouldn't be able to keep my hands off that fine ass.*

LYDIAN: *Tell me more . . .*

KELL: *More about which? The spanking? Or the squeezing? Or the long, hard fucking?*

"Oh." One of the female investors gasps as she reads the screen, her cheeks turning bright pink.

"She's a longtime client," Kell says to her with a devilish wink. "Likes to start the day with dirty talk."

I asked Kell to keep it real without getting crazy explicit, and this is what I had in mind. I want the investors to know exactly what we do here, and that it's not always PG.

"So how long will this convo go on?" one of the Durant twins asks.

Kell shrugs. "Five or ten minutes? Then we'll pick it up again tonight. She's not one for texting while she's at work."

"Tonight?" a gray-haired man in a dark suit asks. "So you'll still be here then?"

"I work 7:00 a.m. to 11:00 a.m. and 7:00 p.m. to 11:00 p.m., six days a week," Kell says. "And the nice thing is I do some of my night shifts from home."

"How many . . . clients do you have?" my former professor asks him.

"Twenty-three." He grins over at me. "But I keep telling Sienna I can take more. There's plenty of Kellan McKenzie to go around."

Kell looks at the female investor then and winks. The man next to her narrows his eyes with dismay. I feel a flare of aggravation at Kell's flirtatiousness. He just can't seem to help himself.

After a little more back-and-forth between Kell and his client, we move into the office of Sam, one of my younger alphas. He's a twenty-six-year-old grad student with short, reddish hair who always seems to be smiling.

"Welcome," he says, nodding to the investors. He turns back

to his screens then, and I see he's balancing a conversation on each of the three computer monitors in front of him.

I read the lines on the first screen:

SAM: *You studied your ass off. I know you're ready.*

SARAHJ: *But what if I didn't study the right things? This professor's exams are hard AF.*

SAM: *That's the voice of doubt creeping in. Tell it to shut up. You're prepared for this.*

SARAHJ: *I think so. I've done everything I possibly could.*

SAM: *Go crush it, gorgeous. Text me when you're done.*

On the second screen, there's a totally different kind of convo going down:

ALICIA1987: *I gave that motherfucker the best years of my life, and THIS IS HOW HE REPAYS ME? By fucking me over in the divorce? I'm surprised he didn't ask me to wipe his new girlfriend's ass while he was at it. He is not getting ANY of the money my grandma left me. She would slap me from beyond the grave if I let that happen. Grammie always hated Mike. She was a smart woman.*

SAM: *You're absolutely right, babe. Can't believe he even has the balls to ask for that after what he did.*

ALICIA1987: *I know, right?? He fucks my best friend and then expects me to smile, give him half of everything, and let them run off into the sunset together? HA, NOT HAPPENING! And he thinks I'm giving him the dog? NO!!!! All he deserves is a hard kick in his droopy nutsack.*

There are a couple soft laughs when investors get to that line. I ignore the third screen and turn to face the group instead.

"So, as you can see, we're filling a void here. Alpha Mail is not just about sex. In fact, it's predominantly not. Most clients just want the emotional support they get from our alphas."

"Is it always the alpha doing the messaging?" an investor in a tailored suit asks me.

"Always. In the interviewing process, we let the guys know that's required. They develop true friendships with these women, and they know what's going on in their day-to-day lives."

"Do you like your work?" an investor asks Sam.

Sam's grin is boyish. "I love it. I get paid to make women happy every day. What could be better than that?"

It's a good note to end the demo on, so I lead the group of investors back to the conference room.

"I can't thank you enough for coming," I tell them, channeling the confidence to finish this presentation strong. "If you have any questions, I'm available now, or you can call me at your convenience."

"And you're looking for immediate buy-in?" an investor asks me.

"We're ready for growth. And I believe we're poised for smart growth that will start to pay off right away."

My heart hammers with anticipation as I look at the faces of the investors. I know not every one of them will buy in, but I'm hoping at least some will. Conventional financing would require more collateral than I have. Alpha Mail will be fine without investors—we'll continue our slow, steady growth. But investment will help us grow now—while the market is ripe and the business is booming.

One of the Durant brothers glances at the other one, who gives him a curt nod. They both turn to me. My heart starts to pound, because this feels like the moment of truth. And then, finally, after a second that feels like a lifetime, one of them says, "We're in."

#besties

BY THE TIME I'm walking up the stairs to my brownstone at the end of investor pitch day, it's dark outside. The faint sounds of laughter from neighbors make me nostalgic for summer evenings spent on my patio with friends before Carmen and Jack moved in.

They were always there—Carmen drinking sangria with the adults while Jack played with the other kids who usually came over. It was a carefree time for all of us, and they'd often stay the night if it got late.

But then Jack started having vision problems, and after a seizure, Carmen found out he was actually losing his sight due to Batten disease. Nothing has been the same since.

I relock the front door behind me after walking in, and I drop my purse and car keys on a table. The sweet smell of Carmen's apple cinnamon muffins makes my stomach growl. Jack loves having her homemade muffins for breakfast, and I do too.

"Hey," I call into the living room, my heels clicking on the oak wood floors that run throughout the brownstone's entire main level.

Carmen is curled up on the couch, her blond hair still damp from the shower. The dark circles under her eyes remind me of our college days, where we met when we were randomly assigned to be roommates in our dorm. Then, Carmen's late nights were due to studying and the occasional night out.

These days, she doesn't sleep well. Even though she and Jack have their own bedrooms, she sleeps with him so she can be there if anything happens. She wakes up in the night often just to check on him.

"Oh, hey." She sits up and gives me a groggy look. "I must've gone to sleep."

She gets up, brushes the hair back from her face and speed-walks across the room and up the stairs to Jack's room. I know she won't be able to concentrate on anything else until she checks on her sleeping son.

I kick off my heels by the couch and walk into the kitchen. It's a modern and traditional mix of warm woods and cool stainless steel. I snag a muffin from the island and bite into it as I open the door to the fridge and scan its contents.

If not for Carmen, I'd have nothing in here but a bottle of wine and maybe some leftover takeout. She keeps the kitchen stocked with healthy food and cooks dinner every night, though I've offered to hire a meal delivery service.

Jack likes helping her with dinner, though, and she's told me many times she needs to keep herself busy because it helps manage the anxiety she feels over his illness.

"Hey," she says, her shoulders dropped into a relaxed position as she walks into the kitchen. "He's good."

"Good. Was it a good day?"

"Yeah." She smiles. "We went to the park and the grocery store."

"And made muffins. I couldn't resist."

"Eat up. I made a double batch. And there's a plate of veggie lasagna in the fridge for you."

"That sounds really good. I'm so hungry."

Carmen slides onto a stool at the island, takes a muffin, and pauses before biting into it. "So, how did it go today? Did you kill it like I knew you would?"

I slide the plate of lasagna into the microwave and start it. "It was good. Better than I even hoped for. The reason I'm so late is because some investors bought in immediately."

"Immediately?" Her face lights up with a smile. "Sienna, I'm so proud of you!"

"Thank you." I lean a hip against the island and meet her gaze. "None of this would be happening without that night of brainstorming over margaritas, you know. I should be thanking you too."

She waves a hand dismissively. "Stop it. Alpha Mail is all you. You've done such an amazing job with it."

"The bigger it gets, the more challenging it will become." The microwave beeps, and I take out my plate. "But I'm ready."

"You should take a vacation. You deserve it."

I sit down on the stool next to hers and look at her. "I can't even take one day off right now, let alone a vacation. You and Jack should go somewhere, though."

Carmen shakes her head adamantly. "No. Please don't surprise me with a vacation or anything, Sienna. I need to be here, where I have Jack's doctors nearby and I know the exact route to the emergency room. He could have a seizure at any time."

Her unsteady voice guts me. Carmen lives every hour of every day for Jack.

"Is there anything I can do?" I offer.

She gives me a sad smile and shakes her head. I know she understands the helplessness I feel. I'd do anything to comfort and help my best friend, if only I could—just like she wishes she could do for Jack.

"Just being here and not having to worry about money is more than I'll ever be able to repay you for," she murmurs, her voice welling with emotion.

"I don't want any repayment. I wouldn't take it if you offered." There's an unintentional note of defensiveness in my tone.

Carmen gives me an apologetic look. "I know." She sighs heavily. "I just can't imagine where we'd be without you. Jack's father is God knows where, and my own family can't be troubled to drive a few hours for a visit."

I take a bite of the lasagna and moan with satisfaction. "This is amazing."

"Yeah? I put more pepper flakes in it this time. And I grated the mozzarella myself."

She grins, a few of the weary lines disappearing from her face. When Carmen gets down, I always listen, but eventually, I find a way to distract her. Worrying about things she can't change doesn't help, and it just makes her feel even worse.

"There's an open house at Coop's station this weekend," I say. "I was thinking we could go. Jack can put on a helmet and sit in one of the trucks."

"Oh, he'd love that. His eyes just light up every time we see a fire truck go by."

My brother will make sure Jack gets the red-carpet treatment. He's the captain of his five-man crew, and the other guys jump at his commands. At least, they do when I'm around. Who knows if they're really that compliant all the time. They're afraid to even make eye contact with me because of all the ways Coop has threatened to kill them if they hit on me.

"How is Coop?" Carmen asks. "Is he still seeing that flight attendant?"

"No. Her voice annoyed him."

She laughs and walks around the island to get a bottle of water from the fridge. "Wasn't her voice the same as it was when he met her?"

I shrug. "I imagine he didn't mind it much when she was screaming his name, but when it came time for actual conversation . . ."

"Ah. So he's still playing the field?"

"More like every field in the league. You know how he is."

This time, it's Carmen who shrugs. "Hey, if you're hot and single and don't want to settle down, there's nothing wrong with that."

"Exactly. I don't want to settle down either, but I'd rather just be alone."

"I think some dashing executive will walk into your office one day and sweep you off your feet."

I roll my eyes and set down my fork. "I don't want to be swept. My feet are just fine on the ground, thank you very much."

"But you won't be able to resist." Her eyes light up as she sets her bottle of water on the island and makes a sweeping gesture that looks like jazz hands. "He'll say, 'Sienna, I want to crunch your numbers, girl. Spread your sheets.'"

We're both laughing, my long day and her sick child forgotten for just a few seconds. It feels good.

"I'm happy on my own," I say when we've both quieted. "I truly am."

"I know." Carmen slides back onto the stool next to me. "You don't *need* a man, that's for sure. But don't you ever *want* one?"

A few seconds of silence pass before I respond. "Not really. I don't have time. And it's just a bunch of nonsense anyway. Most of the men I went out with just wanted sex. They were all about lavish dates where they talked about themselves constantly and thought I'd be so impressed I'd fall into their bed that night."

"Yeah, I don't miss any of that."

"But do you ever wish you had someone?" I ask her. "Someone totally unlike Jack's father?"

She smiles weakly. "Sometimes I think it would be nice just to have a man who would hug me. You know, one of those hugs where you're all wrapped up in big arms and a hard chest and it's so warm you can't help but relax?"

I nod. "A man who will hug you like that without getting hard and trying to have sex with you is a rare find indeed."

"They're out there." Carmen squeezes my hand. "And I hope you find one of them someday. The only man in my life will be waking up by seven, so I'd better get to sleep."

She stands, and I slide off of my stool and reach for her with a hug.

"My arms aren't big and my chest isn't hard, but I'll hug you anytime," I say.

She hugs me back and murmurs, "I love you."

"Love you too. Sleep well."

She walks out of the kitchen, and I relive the day in my mind, physically exhausted but still on cloud nine in my head. Alpha Mail can move to the next level now.

We're fortunate that, for now, Jack's illness is stable. But that could change at any time, and if it does, I want to be ready with the money for nursing care and anything else he needs. Jack is like a nephew to me, and given my brother's love 'em and leave 'em style, he may be the only one I ever have. I want him to have everything he needs, and if I keep growing my business at the rate I'm going, he will.

FOUR

#WTFisthisWTFery

THE NEXT MORNING, there's a new energy in the Alpha Mail offices. Everyone is buzzing about the successful pitch and our impending growth.

Dane, the darkest and broodiest of the alphas on my staff, growls at me as we pass each other in the hallway.

"I hope a decent coffeemaker is part of the office remodel." He narrows his eyes in a glare as he raises his stainless steel mug in the air. "This shit tastes like sewage."

"Doesn't all shit taste like sewage?" I quip.

He's not amused. But at least he keeps his commentary about the old coffeemaker to himself and walks on.

Why women like talking to a guy who seems perennially pissed off is beyond me, but we have clients who love Dane. He's a bartender by night, and he's also a full-time student in business school. Maybe he's always pissed because he's so tired.

When I walk into my office, there's an enormous, exotic-looking vase of flowers on my desk. Bright oranges and pinks are mixed with tropical greenery. I furrow my brow and reach for the white card tucked beneath the vase.

I open it and read the neat, handwritten message.

Congratulations on your successful pitch. I'm very much looking forward to working with you.
—Ben Durant

My brows shoot up in surprise. I look at the flowers again, and then read the words on the notecard one more time.

Is this just a professional courtesy, or something more? I hope it's the former, because I don't need any personal feelings getting in the way of a relationship with an investor. Even one who looks like Ben Durant.

Which one was he, anyway? He and his brother look so much alike, I don't know how anyone can tell them apart. I decide it doesn't matter, move the flowers over to a table in my office, and sit down at my desk.

Jane walks in then, nearly silent as she carries a cup of coffee to my desk and sets it down. I eye the Starbucks cup as I slide on my reading glasses.

"How's our office coffeemaker?" I ask her.

She opens her mouth to respond but closes it again, seemingly lost for words. I smile.

"Can you pick up a new one today?"

"Sure. I would have mentioned it, but we had a freeze on expenses, so . . ."

"No, I understand. I'm going to relax the budget a bit now that our investment came through."

I take a sip of the Pike Place that's my lifeblood. I pay for my Starbucks fixes out of my personal expense account, but I still want to provide good coffee for the staff here.

"These are gorgeous." Jane walks over to the bouquet of

flowers and brushes her fingertips across the petals of an orange flower. "It's not your birthday, though. Some other occasion?"

She's fishing. If there's office gossip, she always wants to be the first to know. And since it's common knowledge that I haven't been on a date in a long time, I can see the wheels turning in her mind. She thinks I've got a man, and she wants to tell the entire office.

I should tell her the truth—that they're just from a colleague. But I kind of like to make her suffer.

"Hmm?" I feign distraction, looking up from my computer. "Oh, not really."

"Was there a card? Or are they from a secret admirer?"

"There was a card."

"Mmm." She leans, searching to see if it's tucked into the blooms.

Too bad for her it's on my desk.

"Let's cater in lunch for everyone today," I say.

"I'll get right on it." With a new task to focus on, Jane turns away from the flowers and heads for the door. "Where would you like me to order from?"

I consider. "How about that deli Gretchen's brother owns? Their food is always good."

"You've got it."

She leaves my office, and I click on the icon to open my email. It takes me almost half an hour to respond to the messages of congratulations on yesterday and interest from investors. There are even messages from investors who weren't here yesterday but heard about it from people who were.

It feels amazing to have so many people eager to sink money into Alpha Mail. Yesterday did go very well, but that was the culmination of years of hard work. And it's not over. The hardest work is likely ahead, as I maximize every dollar and grow the business as wisely as I can.

There's only one message remaining, and it's from an address I don't recognize.

....

To: smills@alphamail.com
From: RoughRider16@bysmail.com
Re: newspaper article

Ms. Mills,

Just wanted to tell you I enjoyed the article in the Sun about your business. You're clearly a driven woman, and I have no doubt Alpha Mail will continue to thrive under your leadership.

However, you've got a few things to learn about the nature of a strong man. You said in the article that you've dated alphas before, but trust me—you haven't.

Roll your eyes all you want. I can help you up the game at your business if you're willing to listen.

Awaiting your response.

....

I furrow my brow, lean back in my chair, and then immediately lean forward to read the unsigned message again. Yep, it's still obnoxious. I shake my head and write back a quick response.

....

To: RoughRider16@bysmail.com
From: smills@alphamail.com
Re: newspaper article

Thanks for your offer, but your advice isn't needed.
Sienna Mills

....

I give the anonymous emailer credit for one thing and one thing only. I *did* roll my eyes as I read his message. I don't claim to be perfect; I built my business through hard work and trial and error. But if there's something I *am* an expert in, it's men who think they know it all.

Time and again, I ran into men like that one. They drank in my body with their eyes and then told me I'd be begging them to do all sorts of filthy things to me in no time flat. Told me they knew my body better than I did. Flexed their muscles and said they wanted to own me. I was actually told not to "worry my pretty little head" once.

There's nothing sexy about being treated like a possession. Having a man lose his shit because another man looked at me isn't hot, it's embarrassing.

Carmen and I are both living proof that women really can do it all on our own. Jack's father, Danny, promised he'd raise their child by Carmen's side and then ditched out right after his birth. And I built my business on my own, with no help from anyone I wasn't paying to work for me.

We both may be perennially exhausted, but it's been years since either of us had a serious relationship, and neither of us wants one. Our emotional support comes from each other.

I've got a best friend I can rely on and a top-of-the-line vibrator I can *also* rely on. That's my definition of fulfillment.

The sweet scent of the nearby flowers drifts over to my desk, and I feel a pang of guilt for dismissing Ben's kind gesture so quickly.

I type out a quick email to him.

....

Ben,

Thanks for the lovely flowers. That was so thoughtful of you. I'm also looking forward to moving Alpha Mail forward in partnership with the investors.

Best,

Sienna

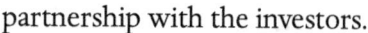

There. I thanked him without making it sound like I'm interested in anything more than a business relationship.

Been there, done that. And if I had a T-shirt, it would say "Over it."

I open an internet browser to start looking for a local interior designer to redecorate Jack's bedroom. He loves *Star Wars*, and I want to surprise him with a makeover.

What drives me these days, other than growing Alpha Mail, is anything that makes Jack smile. I can see why Carmen has lost herself in her son—that gap-toothed grin of his makes me warmer inside than anything ever has.

This is unconditional love. It fuels me and guts me at the same time. Lifts me high into the air and then drops me to the cold, hard ground. Loving Jack is the easiest thing I've ever done, but one day, it's going to break my heart into a million pieces.

Not today, though. Today, I'll keep moving forward, and I'll see the joy around me, just like Jack does.

#notalass

WHEN I GET to my office the next morning, Dane grunts his approval of the new coffeemaker as we pass in the hallway. I'm half smiling when Kell walks by and winks at me.

"Mornin', lass."

"It's Sienna," I remind him—*again.*

My partial smile disappears when I get to my office and open my email. The attorney for Alpha Mail sent me paperwork to review, and one contract is thirty-three pages long. I know what I'll be doing all morning.

There's also another message waiting in my inbox, and it makes me scowl. Though I know it's only going to aggravate me, I can't help opening it anyway, out of sheer curiosity.

....

To: smills@alphamail.com
From: RoughRider16@bysmail.com
Re: so touchy

Sienna,
You must've read my message pre-first cup of coffee yesterday.

You seem too savvy to dismiss quality help when it's offered for nothing.

Do you doubt my prowess? I suppose I understand that. There are lots of men out there who claim to know what turns women on, but most of them are all talk.

I'm not. Here's a piece of advice you can take or leave—your choice. In the Sun article, you said alphas are possessive. I disagree. When I'm with a woman, I don't have to keep my eyes on every other man in the room. I don't have to remind her she's mine. You know why? I'm not insecure. Why would any woman crave a cheap hamburger when she's got prime rib at her disposal?

I've never told a woman she's mine, but I've sure as hell shown a few. A real man shows that with his reverence.

Actions. They set a true alpha apart from a wannabe. You'd know if you'd been with a man like me. I open doors. I pay for dinner. I walk on the side of the road closest to traffic. I get soaked in the rain while holding the umbrella over my partner. I make sure she knows that, to me, she's the only woman in the world.

If you want more advice, you need only ask. I'm at your service.

....

I gasp at my laptop screen, wondering if this is actually one of my friends toying with me. I don't know who would do that. Then again, would an anonymous stranger really be this arrogant and assuming?

Ah. Right. He's a man, so . . . yeah.

I fire back a response.

....

To: RoughRider16@bysmail.com
From: smills@alphamail.com

Dear nameless benefactor,

I suppose you're the prime rib in this scenario? Please don't bother telling me what cuts of meat you assign to your dates. Of which there are dozens—no, hundreds. I get it.

I'm starry-eyed, is that what you want to hear?

....

I hit "Send," exhale deeply, and open the contract. When I read legalese, I go slowly, making sure I'm taking in every sentence and considering the implications. I've marked up the first thirty pages of the document when I look at the clock and realize I've been working on it for more than three hours.

After taking off my reading glasses, I rub my eyes, put the glasses back on, and open my email. And of course, among the messages in my inbox is one from the mystery man.

....

To: smills@alphamail.com
From: RoughRider16@bysmail.com
Re: still touchy

Sienna,

You aren't the first woman I've made starry-eyed. Usually, though, I actually get to see the stars in their eyes. I'll just have to imagine yours.

And no, I haven't dated hundreds of women. In fact, it's been a while since I've had a serious relationship. It's not about quantity. If I'm not with a woman I'm crazy about, I don't want to waste her time or mine.

What about you? You said in the article that your inspiration for Alpha Mail was your own failed love life. Are you really the best person to be helping the lovelorn?

Your cheeks are rosy right now, aren't they? Bet that happens every time you get angry. You're a classic redhead, aren't you? Fiery temper, fierce loyalty, and independent to a fault.

Have a good afternoon. And thanks for acknowledging that I am, in fact, your benefactor.

....

I scoff at my screen with disgust. This guy. I know I shouldn't waste another second of my time on him. He's obviously baiting me and I'm falling for it, but it's like my hands are going to the keyboard without my mind even having a say.

I'm about to send him a scathing response when Jane opens the door to my office and sticks her head into the room, her expression frantic.

"Our server is down."

"We have redundancy. We'll be okay," I tell her.

"We're not okay. There's no internet. None of the alphas can get their messages through on the computers."

I stand up and head out of my office, going straight to the small, freezing cold server room where my two IT guys work.

"We're on it," one of them says as soon as I walk in.

"What's going on?" I ask them.

"We don't know. It's not just us. There has to be a cut cable somewhere or something."

I nod and lean against the doorframe. "What can we do?"

"We're working on it."

By his tone, and the looks of intense concentration on the faces of both IT guys, I can tell they want to be left alone to do their work. And I can understand that. When I'm in the midst of an office crisis, the last thing I want to do is stop and explain it all to someone who doesn't understand.

"Keep me updated," I say, leaving the room.

The internet service interruption ends up dominating my

afternoon. Between upset customers and cranky alphas complaining about having to text old-school by phone—the horror—I'm putting out fires until evening.

I finally make it back to my office a little after 6:00 p.m., when—finally—the internet service is restored. I'm too wiped out to finish the contract or check my email. I haven't even eaten today.

When I pick up my phone and glance at the screen, there's a message from Coop.

COOP: *Hey sis, come hang out with me at Lucky Seven tonight. Haven't seen you in forever.*

He's right; it has been too long. And I'm so hungry that even bar food from the pub the off-duty firefighters frequent will taste good.

I grab my bag and head out of the office, driving my sedan the five miles to Lucky Seven in less than half an hour, which isn't bad considering rush-hour traffic.

The place is a dive, with wood floors, walls covered with vintage beer signs and blaring honky-tonk music. But it has a great vibe—full of warmth and laughter. My older brother calls out my name and slides the brunette off his lap when he sees me approaching.

"Hi, kid." He hugs me, and the brunette gives me a dirty look. "Glad you came."

Coop pulls out a high barstool for me at his table, and I sit down. He heads to the bar to get me a drink, knowing I want a white wine without having to ask, and a blond waitress stops him on his way, batting her eyelashes as she balances a tray full of food in the air.

My brother is a shameless flirt. Though his relationships never last longer than a carton of milk, every new woman seems to think she's the one who will change him. And with his dark, wavy hair, broad shoulders, and blue eyes, he has no trouble attracting new ones.

"Hey, Pup."

I look over my shoulder and smile at my brother's childhood best friend, Ryan. He's known me since I was a little girl with skinned knees and pigtails, trailing around the neighborhood after him and Coop. They said I looked like a lost puppy back then, and the nickname stuck with Ryan. He's like a second older brother to me.

"Hey, you." I give him a quick hug from my barstool.

"Coop said your business is doing well. Good for you."

"Yeah, it's been good. Thanks."

A guy in a navy-blue T-shirt worn by firefighters in Coop's department covers my hand with his on the table.

"Hey, you're Coop's sister? I'm Lorenzo, his—"

"Fuck off," Ryan interjects, making a shooing motion.

"But I'm just—"

Ryan shakes his head. "You don't want him to see you touching his little sister, man, trust me. Fuck off."

Lorenzo looks him over, seeming to decide with Ryan's size that it's not worth challenging him. He leaves, and I give Ryan a look of annoyance.

"Really?"

"You know I'm right."

"I know you're both over the top with the protectiveness. I can take care of myself. And I'm a grown woman, you know? Maybe I'm looking for a date."

Ryan furrows his brow. "Not in a shithole bar, Pup."

Coop returns, handing Ryan a bottled beer and me a glass of wine.

"To my baby sister," he says, holding up his own bottle for a toast. "Kicking ass and taking names. I'm proud of you."

We clink and drink. As Coop slides back onto his stool, I notice his "Oakhurst Football" T-shirt.

"Is that Ryan's team?" I ask him.

He grins. "Yep. I'm an assistant coach."

I look at Ryan, who's also grinning.

"The two of you, together, as role models for high school boys? Wow."

"Hey, now." Ryan cocks a brow at me. "I'm a great coach. Hell, I only got the teaching job at Oakhurst so I could coach this team."

"You two stay away from the cheerleaders." I laugh and take a sip of my wine.

They both give me admonishing looks.

"I wouldn't even consider it," Ryan says. "Those are my students, Sienna."

I know I offended him, because he used my actual name.

"Of course you wouldn't. I was only teasing."

Coop gives me a serious look. "How's Carmen's boy?"

"He's stable, for now. But that could change at any time."

Ryan shakes his head. "That's a hell of a bad deal. And the kid's dad isn't even around, is he?"

"No. But Danny's a deadbeat, so it's better this way. Carmen has me."

Coop crosses his arms over his chest. "Tell her to bring him over to the station anytime. We'll get him a helmet and let him help us cook dinner. Kids always seem to like that."

"Thanks, I will. Or maybe I'll bring him by. Carmen never takes a break. This weekend, I'm going to force her to. Jack and I are going to hang out Saturday."

"So his illness . . . it's bad, isn't it?" Coop's voice is pained.

"Yes," I say softly. "He won't make it out of childhood. But

Carmen is determined to love him for every second she has him."

A few moments of sad silence pass before Ryan says, "If there's anything I can do, let me know. I could put together a fundraiser."

"Thank you. I'm feeling pretty good financially with the business doing so well."

Coop leans his elbows on the table and clears his throat. "You know, Sienna . . . I'm proud of your business and all, but there's nothing that makes me prouder than the way you're sticking by Carmen."

His eyes are a little glassy, and it gets me. I squeeze his hand and clear away the lump in my throat.

"So, you guys, I need some advice."

"If it's about a man, say no," Coop says gruffly.

"Well, it is, but . . . it's not like that." I tuck my hair behind my ear. "There's this guy who has sent me a couple emails about my business. He's telling me I don't really know alphas, and he does."

Coop laughs. "Has he built a successful business with the word 'alpha' in its name?"

"No." I raise my chin a little higher. "I mean, surely not."

"Tell him to fuck off. He's probably just hitting on you anyway."

I roll my eyes. "Coop, you think every man is hitting on me."

"I'm usually right," he mutters.

I turn to Ryan. "What do you think?"

He shrugs. "Tell him to put his money where his mouth is. Put up or shut up, you know?"

"Right."

"Who is this guy, anyway?" Coop scowls. "Someone you know?"

"He doesn't seem to want me to know who he is. He doesn't sign his emails, and his email doesn't have his name in it."

"Is he harassing you? Maybe you should call the cops."

"No, nothing like that."

Coop lowers his brows, looking concerned. "Just be careful. Don't give away anything personal."

"I only sent him my social security number." I wave a hand dismissively.

"Seriously, tell him to fuck off," Coop repeats. "Any guy who's worth a shit will tell you his name."

"Yeah, I suppose you're right."

A waitress approaches the table, and I remember how hungry I am. I grab a menu and order a sandwich, and as soon as she leaves the table, Coop insists I come out to the dance floor with him.

It turns out that dancing with my brother to cheesy country music is just what I needed. The stress of my day is forgotten as we talk and laugh. Very few people can make me so carefree.

By the time Coop and Ryan walk me out to my car a couple hours later, my anonymous adviser is the furthest thing from my mind. All I'm thinking about is getting a good night of sleep so I can hit the ground running tomorrow.

#thisaintmyfirstrodeo

WHEN I WALK into the kitchen sleepy-eyed the next morning, Jack is standing at the kitchen table, giving me a lopsided grin that melts my heart.

"Morning, Jack man." I ruffle his sandy brown hair.

"We have a surprise for you," he says, his smile widening.

He steps aside to reveal a plate on the kitchen table with a stack of pancakes. There's a folded napkin beside the plate with a knife and a fork on it and a glass of orange juice nearby. The paper on the table that says, "Good morning, Sienna" in Jack's block handwriting is my favorite part.

"This is for me?" I give him my most excited expression, mouth open and eyes wide.

He nods and pulls out my chair for me.

My heart swells as I sit down. I shove down the sadness that tries to rise to the surface. This isn't a sad moment, it's a joyful one, and I'll only feel the joy. Jack is here with us right now. He's happy. That's a gift to be treasured.

"Apple cinnamon pancakes," Carmen says, walking over and setting a tiny pitcher of warm syrup on the table.

She's wearing sweats and a T-shirt, her hair in a messy bun, and Jack is wearing his favorite Darth Vader pajamas. I wish I could stay here with them all day, cuddled up under a blanket watching movies, but I have to go to work.

"Are you guys going to eat with me?"

Jack's expression turns sober. "I was really hungry. I already ate."

I laugh and ruffle his hair again. "No worries. You'll sit and talk to me, though, right?"

"Yeah."

He takes the chair across from mine and animatedly recaps a *Star Wars* movie he watched last night. Something about a volcano and light sabers. No matter how many times he watches those movies, he never gets tired of them.

I finish breakfast, take a shower, and dress in a simple dark purple dress and black booties. I'm later than usual getting into the office, and when I walk into the lobby, I see one of the Durant brothers standing near the elevator. He's wearing a crisp, charcoal suit with a pale blue dress shirt, his thick, dark hair just unruly enough to look sexy and polished at the same time.

As I approach him, I see he's talking to Rob, a very popular alpha on my staff. Rob is built with muscles that are covered in tattoos. He's bald, with intense blue eyes. Last year, I found out several of his clients were mailing him their panties, and he was storing them in one of his desk drawers. I was disgusted and slightly impressed at the same time, because from what I heard, they were all *worn* panties. So. Gross.

"Sienna." The Durant brother turns to me as I approach, giving me a warm smile.

"Ben." I venture a guess that the one who sent the flowers is the one who took the time to come back to the office.

I must be right. Ben nods, gives me a quick, appreciative glance and then turns back to Rob.

"Rob was just telling me about his daughter."

I laugh and arch my brows. "Lexi? We love it when she comes to visit."

"She's my whole world, wrapped up in a precocious little package." Rob's eyes take on the affectionate glow I only see when he talks about the four-year-old girl he's a single dad to.

"I didn't mean to keep you," Ben says to Rob, glancing at his wrist, where a chunky, expensive-looking watch sits. "I know you said you have to get to your office."

"No worries." Rob extends his hand to shake Ben's. "It was good talking to you, man."

Rob smiles and nods at me, then walks away, leaving me alone with Ben.

"So . . ." He gives me a smile that almost looks nervous, but he quickly regains his composure. "I wanted to ask you out for breakfast to go over the expansion plans, but I don't have your cell number."

"Ah, right. Sorry about that." I clear my throat. "It's . . . I mean, I can email it to you if that works so you can text next time?"

He nods, a flicker of disappointment passing over his face. "You don't have time right now, then?"

"I already ate, actually."

"I understand. Rain check?"

His genuine disappointment touches something inside me. I take out my phone, open my email, and send him my cell number.

"I just sent you my number. And maybe we could do breakfast Monday? There's a great little bakery a block over."

"Perfect. I'll text you, then."

"Okay. And thank you again for the flowers."

"It was my pleasure, Sienna."

As Ben steps away, I get a whiff of his cologne, which smells quite nice. I haven't spent time with a man outside the office in so long that I'd forgotten what a man smells like close up.

I walk back to my office, eager to get started on the workday since I'm running late.

As soon as I open my email, my light mood evaporates when I see the message I read yesterday but never responded to. I read it again and am as incensed as I was the first time. Before I can even think about whether or not I should, I'm writing back.

....

To: RoughRider16@bysmail.com
From: smills@alphamail.com
Re: unimpressed

Dear RoughRider (since you don't have the balls to tell me your actual name),

My benefactor? Please. So far, you've taught me exactly nothing. Also, you're arrogant, which I'm sure is just one of your many lovely qualities.

I mean, seriously—RoughRider? Because you'll give me the roughest, most satisfying ride of my life, right? Yawn. Heard it all before. Still prefer to stay single.

What about the 16 on your email address, though? Shouldn't that be a 69? Wink, wink, nudge, nudge.

This ain't my first rodeo, RoughRider. I've dated men like you before. Go find someone who will be wowed when you flex for her. If you even have any muscles, that is.

Sienna

....

Shortly after I send the message, my inbox dings with a

response.

....

To: smills@alphamail.com
From: RoughRider16@bysmail.com
Re: apologies

Dear Sienna,

I must apologize. I think my efforts at playful banter have made you think I'm someone I'm not. I'm genuinely not arrogant, and believe it or not, there's no sexual innuendo in my email address.

It's hard to convey tone by email. I didn't mean to offend you.

If you'd like me to write again, say so. If not, I won't bother you again.

RoughRider

....

I sit back in my chair, my brow furrowed with surprise. I wasn't expecting that. RoughRider is capable of contrition?

All I need to do now is not respond. Like he said, he won't bother me again. I'm still thinking about it when Jane comes into my office, fresh Starbucks in hand.

"Have I told you lately that I love you?" I give my assistant a grateful smile as she passes me the cup.

She returns my smile, but hers looks a little nervous. "Remember that fifteen seconds from now."

"Oh, geez." I sigh heavily. "What is it?"

"Client Services is having an issue with a client, and they need you to weigh in."

"Tell Anthony he needs to run his own department. He's a manager; he needs to manage. I've told him I'll stand behind any call he makes."

Jane arches her brows, considering her next words.

"Well . . . Anthony is kind of out of ideas on this one."

I take off my reading glasses and turn away from my desk to face my assistant. "Okay, can you tell me more?"

"From what Anthony told me, a client says she's in love with one of the alphas. He's stuck to the company boundaries, but she wants more and she's become quite . . . aggressive about it."

"Can you be more specific?"

"She's mailed him nude photos of herself, and she was waiting for him in his car when he left work the other day, and she was, um . . . nude then too."

"Eww." I cringe, and Jane's expression relaxes a little.

"It gets worse," she says. "Last night, she followed him home from work, and when he got there, she confronted him at his front door and showed him a tattoo of his name on . . . one of her buttocks."

Poor Jane. I recruited her from a tech firm. By her flaming cheeks, I can tell she never expected to be giving her boss a report about anyone's ass tattoo.

"Okay, I'll go talk to Anthony about it," I tell her. "Thanks for letting me know."

Anthony is relieved when I walk into his office, where he's meeting with the alpha in question, Isaac.

"I didn't have the heart to tell her my name was spelled wrong on the tat," he says sheepishly.

"You looked at it?" I give him a stern look.

He puts his hands up in defense. "She dropped her pants on my front porch and turned around. It was right in my face."

"You need to call the police," I tell Anthony. "You wrote up reports on this from the beginning, right?"

Anthony nods, and I sigh with relief. "Good."

"I wasn't sure you'd want the police involved because of the potential for bad PR," Anthony says.

I look at Isaac, a handsome blond who was one of my first hires. "Have you crossed any lines with her? Done anything to encourage this behavior? You need to be completely honest right now."

"No. I need this job. You've been good to me, and I follow all the rules. I've got a girlfriend, and even if I didn't, I wouldn't hook up with a client."

"What did you do when you found her in your car?"

He shakes his head. "Well, after I had a fuckin' heart attack because there was a naked person in my back seat, I told her she had to go. That I have a girlfriend and it can't be like that with us."

"And did she?"

"No. She started . . . you don't want to know, trust me. I left my car there and caught a cab home. The security guys checked it for me the next day."

"And she was gone?"

Isaac nods. "But she left a dildo in my car. A *used* dildo."

"Oh, shit." I clear my throat. "Sorry. That just slipped out."

"I said 'dildo,' so I think you're allowed to say 'shit.'" Isaac shrugs.

"Have the interior of your car cleaned, and we'll take care of the bill. Anthony will work with the police to resolve this." I turn to my Client Services Director. "And obviously, we're dropping her as a client."

We talk for a few more minutes, and when I'm walking back to my office, I can't help laughing a little. There's never a dull moment at Alpha Mail.

I sit back down at my desk and put my glasses on. The email from RoughRider is still up on my computer screen, and after reading it again, I feel an urge to respond. There's something about him. He's not put off by my bluntness, as people sometimes are.

And he can take it as well as he dishes it out, apparently.

I decide to write him back.

....

To: RoughRider16@bysmail.com
From: smills@alphamail.com
Re: apologies

Dear RoughRider,

Apology accepted. And I apologize for being so harsh.

So who are you, really? Why the secrecy?

I don't suppose any advice can hurt, so go ahead and hit me with some. You said true alphas aren't possessive, and I'm not sure I buy that, but I'm open to new ideas.

Sienna

....

I go about my workday, leaving for a meeting out of the office and then lunch with a friend from college, and when I get back to my office that afternoon, there's a message waiting in my inbox.

....

From: RoughRider16@bysmail.com
To: smills@alphamail.com
Re: fresh start

Sienna,

Your apology wasn't needed. I like your fire. Never change.

A man who's loving his woman the right way doesn't have to worry about other guys. He lives to make her laugh, to listen, and to be her shoulder to cry on. He knows her like no other man does—her favorite drink, how she likes to unwind, and what makes her beg for mercy in the bedroom. No stranger can compete with that.

A true alpha takes care of his girl—body, heart, and soul. The wannabes are all swagger, and maybe you've been fooled by them in the past. But there are real men like me out there, and we'd walk through fire for the woman we love.

I can't tell you who I am. Does my name even matter all that much? The things I wrote above in this email—that's who I am.

So tell me a little something about who you are. Not the ass-kicking CEO, but the woman inside. Who are you, really, Sienna?

RoughRider

....

My pulse is racing when I finish reading the message. I'm surprised by my reaction. The man who pissed me off with his every word just made me feel . . . warm inside.

I'm definitely writing back. But I'm going to make him wait until tomorrow. Which is good, because I may need until then to come up with an answer to his question.

Who am I, really? I'm not actually sure.

SEVEN

#likeaporcupine

CARMEN BENDS DOWN to inspect a pile of zucchini, sniffing it when she's just a couple inches above it.

"Does it smell right for your recipe?" I arch my brows with amusement.

"Maybe." She frowns at the stack of vegetables, considering.

We're on our weekly Saturday morning visit to the local farmers market, where Carmen creates recipes in her head upon seeing the organic vegetables, homemade pasta, and exotic seasonings on display.

"With the right meat . . ." Carmen mumbles, cupping her chin as she considers.

Jack gives me a frantic look as strawberry ice cream trails down the sides of his giant waffle cone, melting despite his efforts to eat it fast.

"Emergency lick!" he cries, passing me the cone.

I grab it, ignoring the stickiness as I wrap my hand around it and lick away the meltiest parts.

"Thanks," he says as I pass it back.

"I feel like I should be the one thanking you." I rub my hand on my jeans in an effort to wipe away some of the stickiness, to no avail. "That's really good ice cream."

Carmen decides to pass on the zucchini, and we move on to the next booth.

"So, if you were trying to describe me, what would you say?" I ask her.

She gives me a confused glance. "To describe you?"

I nod.

"Smart, beautiful, compassionate—"

I cut her off. "Not like that. But thanks, those are all very nice things to say. I guess what I mean is, who do you think I am, deep down?"

She considers. "I think that, deep down, you aren't as cynical as you let on. You're deeply loyal. You value yourself based on professional accomplishments."

"Really?"

"Mostly. Sometimes I think you forget there's a woman inside you who gets scared and hopeful and moody just like the rest of us. You try to be 'on' all the time and never show any weakness."

I knit my brows together and think about her words. My instinct is to rebut them, but I force myself not to. Carmen knows me better than anyone. Maybe there's some truth to what she's saying.

"Why do you ask?" Carmen turns to me, a green pepper in hand.

"Hmm? Oh, just . . . wondering, I suppose."

Carmen squeezes the pepper in several places, then gives it a quizzical look.

"Oh my God, just buy the damn thing." I shake my head. "You fondled it already, might as well make an honest pepper out of it."

She laughs as I pass a couple bucks to the guy running the stand. "Squeezing produce is as close as I get to—" she glances at

Jack "—*you know* . . . these days."

"Tell me about it." I sigh. "I didn't think I cared anymore."

Carmen gives me a side-eye as we walk to the next booth. She doesn't even notice the college-aged guy checking her out as he walks past us. "But . . . ? I know there's more to that statement."

I shrug. "But lately, I guess I've realized I do care some."

"What made you realize that?"

"What are you, my therapist?"

"Obviously. I have been for almost a decade now. And you're mine."

I smile. "I guess just all the men who have been in and out of the office lately."

"As opposed to every other day, when the office is already full of hot men? There has to be one in particular, Sienna. Don't make me drag it out of you."

"There's this guy I'm emailing with, but it's nothing."

"You wouldn't have mentioned it if it was nothing," Carmen says under her breath.

I ignore her and continue. "Remember me telling you about Ben Durant, the one who sent me flowers?"

"Tall, dark, handsome, and rich?"

"Pretty much."

"So go out with him."

I groan. Jack passes me the cone for another emergency lick, and I snag a bite of the waffle cone while I'm at it, then hand it back to him.

"You know how I feel about dating," I remind Carmen.

"But I also know you aren't as cynical as you let on, remember?"

"You really think I should go out with him?"

"I really do." Carmen stops to check out a display of home-made pastas infused with vegetables. "Or the email guy. Or—" she grins and arches her brows "—both."

"The email guy won't tell me who he is."

That stops Carmen cold. "What the hell? Is he a creep?"

I shrug. "Could be. I don't really know."

"Well, how does he seem?"

I furrow my brow as I think about that. "At first . . . like a hole that starts with the letter 'A.'" We've come up with creative ways to swear around Jack. "And then . . . intriguing, I guess. Mysterious."

"Maybe he's *mysterious* because he's married. Or in prison. Or seventy years old. Or . . ." Carmen gives me a serious look. "All of the above."

I half laugh and half sigh. "Maybe. He doesn't seem that way, though."

"Tell him you need to know who he is. He could be a pimply kid emailing you from the bedroom of his parents' house, Sienna."

I cringe and then instinctively look at Jack to make sure he's okay. He is, other than the strawberry ice cream smeared all over his nose and chin.

While Carmen buys some pasta, I bend down and wipe off Jack's face with a napkin.

"How was the ice cream, buddy?"

"Good."

"What else do you want to do today?"

"Go to the park?"

I nod. "Let's do it."

"And can we get pizza from that one place with the white and orange cheese?"

"Absolutely."

Carmen frowns at us as she walks over. "Pizza? I was going to make carbonara tonight."

"Make it tomorrow night," I suggest. "Jack and I are thinking pizza and a movie tonight. He wants to watch a princess movie."

"Sienna! No, I don't!" Jack objects dramatically and smacks his forehead.

"Oh, I thought you loved princesses."

"No." He shakes his head and gives his mom a *can you believe this* look.

"What else could we watch?" I feign bewilderment.

"*The Force Awakens!*"

"Doesn't it have a princess? I *knew* you loved princesses."

Jack's eyes widen as he gives me a serious look. "No, she's a general."

"Are you sure?"

"Yes."

"Hmm. Okay, I still like it."

On our walk home, I'm still thinking about the question posed by my would-be alpha adviser. We put away our purchases and then walk to the park a couple blocks over from my apartment. Jack wears himself out, and when we're back home and he and Carmen fall asleep on the couch, I tiptoe up to my bedroom and call Coop.

"Sienna? Everything okay?"

"Yeah, everything's good. How are you?"

He gives me a noncommittal grunt. "Been working lots of overtime. The money's great, but I'm beat."

"Are you working now?"

"Nah, I finally got a day off. I don't feel like doing anything, though. What's up with you, little sister?"

I sigh heavily and lie down on my bed. "Who do you think I am, Coop?"

"Uh . . . my sister? Is this a trick question?"

"Deep down inside. What moves me? What am I passionate about?"

Another disinterested grunt. "Chick flicks? Apple fritters?"

"Those are things I like, but not who I am. You've known me my whole life. Who am I?"

"How the hell should I know?"

I groan with frustration. "You're so not helpful."

"I never said I was." I can hear his dismissal of this topic in his tone. "Oh, hey, I need a favor."

"What?"

"There's a firefighter's charity ball thing in a few weeks, and I need you to come with me."

I laugh. "Why? It's not like you can't find a real date."

"Yeah, I *can*, I just don't want to. Every woman I go out with lately wants to know where I see things heading with us before we get to fucking dessert."

"To your bedroom, right?"

"Well, yeah," he says sheepishly, "but I can't admit that. Why can't women just have some fun on the first date and see where it leads?"

My "hmm" is skeptical. "Why can't men just be honest about what they really want?"

After a couple seconds of silence, Coop sighs and says, "Anyway, will you come to the thing?"

"Sure. Maybe I'll find some hot firefighters to hook up with."

"Shut up."

I keep going, because I love aggravating Coop. "You'll introduce me to the hot ones, right? A girl has needs, you know."

"Stop, Sienna. You're my sister. I don't want to hear about that shit. And I'll make sure all the guys know you're off-limits, so don't even try it."

"Text me the date so I can add it to my schedule. And if you want us to be matchy-matchy, I'll be wearing a white dress that's see-through on the top. It leaves *nothing* to the imagination."

My brother groans with disgust. "Don't you dare."

"I don't even own a dress like that, Coop. Don't worry, I'll be wearing my habit."

"That's more like it."

"All right, get back to doing nothing."

"Yep. Love you, sis."

"Love you too."

We hang up, and I stare at the ceiling for a couple minutes before reaching over to my bedside table to grab my laptop. I sit up, open the computer, and log on to my work email.

....

To: RoughRider16@bysmail.com
From: smills@alphamail.com
Re: who I am

Dear RoughRider,

Are you having a good weekend? Mine is good so far.

I've been thinking about what you asked me. I think I'll need to answer this question slowly. So here's the beginning of my answer.

I love Oreo cookies (dunked in milk until they're FALLING APART) and cheesy romantic comedies. I'm terrible at all sports. I get grossed out when anyone else uses my toilet.

I'm practical. My lingerie drawer is filled with comfortable, supportive nude-colored bras and butt-covering nude-colored briefs. And while I love shoes and handbags as much as the next woman, I shop at upscale consignment stores for most of my wardrobe.

I'm like a porcupine. The quills are my outer persona—tough and strong and ready for battle. Not only am I comfortable in a conference room with nothing but back-slapping men, I'm in my element there. Kicking ass and taking names in a corporate setting is my jam. But what many people don't know is that porcupines' most vulnerable part is their soft underbelly. My soft underbelly is the way I feel about the people I love. There's someone in particular—a little boy—whom I love with my whole heart and soul. But that love comes with a sense of helplessness and hurt that I sometimes can't process, because he's sick. I cry for him at night, when I'm alone. I'd give up everything to help him if I could.

I'm making myself sound better than I am. The truth is, I'm not sure I'd be a good mom if I had my own kids. I'm pretty focused on myself. And when I have PMS . . . well, watch out world.

Your turn. Who are you? And if RoughRider isn't sexual, what's it about?

Sienna

EIGHT

#oreosarealwaystheanswer

To: smills@alphamail.com
From: RoughRider16@bysmail.com
Re: who I am

Dear Sienna,

The Rough Riders reference is a nod to Roosevelt's Rough Riders, the 1st US Volunteer Cavalry, which was formed for the Spanish-American War. It was a diverse group that included college athletes, miners, outdoorsmen, and cowboys.

My weekend was good. I had to work, but I love my work, so I didn't mind. I'm with you on the Oreos, and between you and me, I don't mind a romantic comedy myself.

Your porcupine reference is funny. I know some people think a strong woman who can get shit done is prickly, but those people are (forgive my language) fucking stupid. I wouldn't mind hearing more about your soft underbelly, or your lingerie. Doesn't matter what color it is anyway. The best part of lingerie to a man is the way it feels. When we slide our hands over a woman's ass and cup it through that silky fabric . . . yeah, it's good. And that feeling a guy gets when he unhooks a woman's bra is basically like a chorus of angels singing from above.

I'm sorry about the sick boy you mentioned. Kids shouldn't have to go through that stuff.

You asked who I am, so here goes . . . I'm decisive. I knew what I wanted to do for a career in high school, and as I said before, I love it. Sometimes I think I'm a little too driven, but other times I think I need to step it up. My outlets are exercise and reading.

Being decisive is both good and bad. I know what I want, but that doesn't always mean I can have it.

A real man isn't fazed by PMS. I'd handle yours by listening while massaging your shoulders. And of course—Oreos.

RoughRider

....

To: RoughRider16@bysmail.com
From: smills@alphamail.com
Re: UGH

Dear RoughRider,

I feel like a real ass for assuming your name was a sexual reference. Of course, it had to be noble and patriotic to make me feel even worse.

Moving on . . . What do you do for work? And what do you want that you can't have?

I thought about our alpha conversation this morning because as I was walking into my office, a guy passing me on the street told me my hair would look really good wound around his fingers. He was rubbing his crotch as he said it. Isn't that an alpha attribute? Walking right up to a mark and telling her how rough and good you want to give it to her? Isn't that supposed to make me weak-kneed? Because I thought it was gross, and I told him so.

You aren't married, are you? Or underage? Please tell me I'm not emailing a teenager right now.

Sienna

....

To: smills@alphamail.com
From: RoughRider16@bysmail.com
Re: UGH

Sienna,

You can relax, I'm not a teenager. I'm 32. And I'm not married either.

I don't have long, but I had to write back immediately to set you straight on something. What that guy did to you this morning does not make him an alpha—it makes him a sleazy douchebag. Words like those aren't meant for a woman you see on the street. Men should only say things like that to a woman they're with, and only when they're alone. But I'm not sure I'd even say it then. I prefer actions to words.

Slap the next guy who talks to you that way.

RoughRider

....

To: RoughRider16@bysmail.com
From: smills@alphamail.com
Re: retrospect

RoughRider,

I may slap that guy if I see him on the street again. Do you ever hear something come out of someone's mouth, but there's a delay before your brain registers how offended you actually were by it? I had one of those moments this morning.

This afternoon, I have to fire an employee. I'm dreading it

because I know she genuinely needs this job, but she did something I can't overlook. She has access to money here, and our auditors discovered that she took some money late last year and then replaced it the next month. She probably needed that money for Christmas. Firing people is the worst part of my job, but I think it's important that I do it rather than my HR manager. Everyone deserves to be fired by someone who doesn't relish doing it and who will do it as compassionately as possible. I'm giving her a severance, which I don't have to do. And she stole from the company, so why do I still feel so terrible? My underbelly is showing.

Sienna

....

To: smills@alphamail.com
From: ben.durant@durantholdings.com
Re: say yes

Hey Sienna, are you free for breakfast tomorrow?

....

To: ben.durant@durantholdings.com
From: smills@alphamail.com
Re: say yes

Hi Ben,
Yes.
Sienna

....

To: smills@alphamail.com
From: ben.durant@durantholdings.com
Re: say yes

Meet me at Thistle at 7?

....

To: ben.durant@durantholdings.com
From: smills@alphamail.com
Re: say yes

See you then.

....

To: smills@alphamail.com
From: RoughRider16@bysmail.com
Re: long day

Sienna,

Sorry I'm late getting back to you—it was a long day, and I'm just now getting a chance to sit down and write you.

I'm loving this view of your underbelly, btw. It's very sexy.

How did it go with your employee? I wouldn't relish firing someone who needed the job either. But you're right—you had no choice. She could have come to you and asked for a loan if times were tough, and while you may not have said yes, at least that would have been above board. Hope your day got better when that was over. Heavy is the head that wears the crown.

I have a work dilemma myself, though it's less weighty than yours. Someone I supervise is more deserving of a promotion than the person I have to give it to. I'll call the person I'm giving it to Bob. Bob is arrogant and immature, but he's very good at what he does. He'll execute this role better. The other person, whom I'll call John, works his ass off but just doesn't have the natural talent Bob does. I lifted heavy tonight at the gym because I've been conflicted about this even though I know what I have to do. I realized Bob will win this battle, but John will win far more battles in his life than Bob will. There's no substitute for heart.

It would have been nice to have a late dinner with you tonight after our shitty days. You're beautiful in the skirts and heels you wear to work, with your makeup done, but I bet you're even more beautiful in sweats and a T-shirt, with your hair down, a glass of wine in hand, and a relaxed expression on your face.

A real man doesn't let his girl go to sleep stressed or upset. I know of some great ways to work out stress before bed. But if you just needed me to listen and hold you, I'd do that instead. I'd be the luckiest bastard in the world if I got to be the one to do that.

Sleep well, Sienna.

RoughRider

NINE

#talldarkandinterested

WHEN I WALK into Thistle, I see Ben sitting at a corner table, his arm around the back of the chair next to him as he gazes out the window. With his suit jacket hanging behind him, I can see that his white dress shirt is bright and crisp, and it's accented by a dark red tie. His hair is once again begging me to run my hands through it.

My heels click on the tile floor as I approach the table, and he looks up, smiles, and stands.

"Good morning," he says as I slide into my chair.

"Good morning."

Once I'm seated, he sits back down, still grinning at me. After a second of silence, he says, "You look great."

"Thank you."

The waitress comes over immediately to get our orders, and I take a quick look at the menu before ordering coffee and wheat toast. Ben orders an omelet with extra bacon and toast, giving me a sheepish look when the waitress departs.

"I did a long run this morning," he says. "I don't normally eat that much."

"So you're a morning person?"

He shrugs. "I've realized I kind of have to be. I end up working late most nights, and I don't get workouts in if I don't do them first thing."

"Do you like your work?" I give the waitress a nod and a smile as she sets down our mugs of coffee.

"I love it."

"How long have you guys been in business?"

"Since we finished grad school. We were twenty-six then, so . . . six years?"

I'm connecting some dots, and I feel a swirling sensation in my belly. I realized when I read last night's message that RoughRider seems to be a man who has seen me in real life. Ben exercises, loves his work, and is thirty-two years old. All those things sound very familiar to me. Could he possibly be RoughRider?

"Remind me how old you are?" he says.

"Twenty-eight."

He gives me an appreciative look. "You've accomplished a lot for someone who's not even thirty yet."

"Thanks."

"There's nothing I find sexier than a woman with drive."

I give him a mischievous smile. "Not even a lacy, little thong?"

Ben's brows arch, and the corners of his lips turn up in a smile. "Are you free for a date this weekend?"

I pretend to consider. "I might be free Saturday night."

"What can I do to persuade you for sure?"

"Hmm . . . if I am free, what do you have in mind?"

For the first time in I can't remember how long, I'm flirting. And it feels good. Ben is hot and smart, and even though we're right across from each other at the table, I want to be closer to him. The thought that he's trying to woo me on the side adds even more sex appeal.

But why? What would make him do that? I know I need to keep my suspicion under wraps and see how things play out. But at this moment, not only am I hoping Ben is my mystery man, I'm also hoping he really is a rough rider.

"Dinner at Nobu and dessert at my place." Ben holds my gaze as he tells me about his plans for us.

He's not beating around the bush. I like that. If I accept this date with him, he's hoping it will end with the two of us sweaty, exhausted, and tangled in his bedsheets.

"Okay." I smile at him, hoping for the very same thing.

I'M STILL FEELING warm and excited when I walk into my office forty-five minutes later. That is, until I see a uniformed Chicago Police Department officer and two other men in suits standing by Jane's desk.

"There she is," Jane says, smiling nervously.

Fuck. My first thought is that somehow, things were worse with the employee I fired than I realized. Did she somehow trigger a police investigation with her creative money mismanagement? I can't afford any bad press right now, with new investors freshly onboard.

"Ms. Mills," one of the men in a suit says, extending his hand. "I'm Detective Aidan Pierce. Do you have time for a few questions?"

I've done nothing wrong, but I still feel my blood pressure rising by the second. What if something happened to one of my parents? Or to Coop?

"Of course, come on in." I lead the way into my office, and Jane scurries over to close the door.

"Feel free to grab a seat." I gesture at the chairs in front of my desk and the loveseat along the wall.

"Thanks, but we won't be long," Detective Pierce says.

He looks about my age, with serious brown eyes and the trim physique of a runner.

"Is everything okay?" I ask, unable to stand the suspense any longer.

"Absolutely. We don't mean to alarm you. I would have called to schedule an appointment, but we were in the neighborhood."

"No problem at all." I lean against the corner of my desk, waiting for him to tell me why they're here.

"We'd like to access some of your company records. Communications between Isaac Carter and Isabella Moore."

I nod with realization, and my shoulders drop with relief. "The woman who was stalking him?"

"Right. We need to collect the evidence from here, if possible. If we can access all communications between the two of them, that would be ideal."

"Absolutely. Anything we can do to help. I appreciate you guys taking this seriously."

"Miss Moore was arrested, but she posted bond, so make sure Mr. Carter has security."

"We have. I have someone with him when he leaves his home, and I have surveillance on him at night."

The detective nods and looks at the door. "Can we take a look at those records right now?"

"Sure. I'll have Jane take you over and tell everyone to share anything you need."

I walk over to open the door, stopping with my hand on the handle. "Uh . . . I feel like I should let you guys know that some of the work we do here is . . . sexually explicit. It's all between consenting adults, but . . . you know, there's dirty talk and such."

The other detective tries to hide his grin, and Detective Pierce meets my eyes with a reassuring look. "I'm a Marine, ma'am.

Nothing I haven't seen and heard before. And I'll cover these guys' ears and eyes if needed."

We all share a nervous chuckle, and I take them out to Jane's office and explain to her what's going on. She looks relieved as she gets up to offer them coffee and be their ambassador. Did she think I was getting arrested or something? The thought amuses me.

As soon as I sit down at my desk, my first urge is to write an email to RoughRider. I decide to give in to it.

....

To: RoughRider16@bysmail.com
From: smills@alphamail.com
Re: good morning

Dear RoughRider,

How's prison life? I figure that's probably your big secret. Can't tell me who you are because you're currently living in a cell.

I really shouldn't be as open as I'm being with someone who could be, well . . . anyone, but I'm one of those people who doesn't hold back. It's not like I've given you my ATM PIN or anything, right? You do know about the color of my lingerie and my affinity for soggy Oreos, though. Please don't tell your cellmate.

Your message last night was really nice. I'm curious, though, is that you talking to me or you showing me how a real alpha talks?

Hope your day is going well. Try not to get shanked before you write me back.

S

....

Within five minutes, my inbox dings with a response.

....

To: smills@alphamail.com

From: RoughRider16@bysmail.com
Re: good morning

Good morning to you too. That's quite a theory you have, but fortunately, I'm not in prison. I've never even gotten a speeding ticket. See the halo glowing above my head right now?

I'm glad you liked my message. As to your question—it was both. Me talking to you and showing you how a real alpha talks are one and the same.

Since I hypothetically held you and we talked until we fell asleep last night, this morning you would have woken up to me kissing your neck and letting my hands slowly roam every inch of you. You'd feel your effect on me pressed definitively against your thigh. I'm a patient man, and I'd wait to go further until you were breathing hard and begging for more.

I'd tell you about the rest in great detail, but I've got to get to work. You probably don't want to hear about it anyway.

RoughRider

....

TEN

#letsgetfoxy

To: RoughRider16@bysmail.com
From: smills@alphamail.com
Re: good morning

Dear RoughRider,

Ha. Did you forget that sexy words are the very foundation of my business? If I wanted to hear dirty talk, I've got plenty of options, not to mention a vivid imagination of my own. I know how to lie back, close my eyes, and fantasize about how much I love the feel of a man giving it to me exactly how I like it.

I'd tell you how that is, but you probably know already, right, Pussy Whisperer?

S

PS: How much do I love owning a company where I can send out emails like this knowing IT won't blink an eye? Dirty is our status quo. That sounds like a great ad line . . .

....

To: smills@alphamail.com
From: RoughRider16@bysmail.com

Re: a good morning indeed

Hey, thanks for making me so . . . enthused at work. That's never happened before. I had to sit behind my desk for a few minutes after reading that last message.

And I'm no Pussy Whisperer—no relationships in a while, remember? But yeah, I bet I do know how you like it. Slow and sensual at first, building and building—so damn good, getting faster, until you're close to the edge, and then slowing way down until you're whimpering for more. Faster again, and then slow, so slow, until you're so worked up that just a couple long, hard thrusts finally get you there. And it's good, yeah? I'd ask you even though I already knew, just so I could hear you say yes in that satisfied purr of yours.

Don't try to tell me you didn't like that. Those guys you employ may do it for most women, but not you. I'm the only one you wanted to hear that from. And you're the only one I want to say it to.

RoughRider

....

To: RoughRider16@bysmail.com
From: smills@alphamail.com
Re: a good morning indeed

There are lots of things I'd like to say right now, but I'm going to keep this simple, because when I ask multiple questions, you're adept at avoiding some of them. So I'm only asking one.

Have we met before?

S

....

To: smills@alphamail.com

From: RoughRider16@bysmail.com
Re: a good morning indeed

Sorry it took me so long to answer—work was calling.
Yes, we've met before.
RoughRider

....

To: RoughRider16@bysmail.com
From: smills@alphamail.com
Re: Another question

That worked well—let's do it again. Are you keeping your identity a secret because we have a work relationship of some kind?
S

....

To: smills@alphamail.com
From: RoughRider16@bysmail.com
Re: Another question

No more details. I just wanted you to know I'm not some random crazy guy.

....

To: smills@alphamail.com
From: RoughRider16@bysmail.com
Re: okay then

So you're a known crazy guy. I feel much better now.

....

To: smills@alphamail.com
From: RoughRider16@bys.com
Re: okay then

Do I seem crazy to you? Really?

....

To: RoughRider16@bysmail.com
From: smills@alphamail.com
Re: okay then

No, I'll admit you don't. Will you tell me if you're one of my investors?

....

To: smills@alphamail.com
From: RoughRider16@bysmail.com
Re: no

I said no more details, woman. And to clarify, that subject line means no, I won't tell you.

....

To: RoughRider16@bysmail.com
From: smills@alphamail.com
Re: you're infuriating

You did not just call me "woman." When you can pick your knuckles up from the ground long enough to write out a response, at least tell me what the 16 in your screen name stands for.

....

To: smills@alphamail.com
From: RoughRider16@bysmail.com
Re: giving in

Okay, I'll tell you. It's the number of years left in my sentence.

....

To: RoughRider16@bysmail.com
From: smills@alphamail.com
Re: so funny

Ha. While I do love being toyed with and left in the dark, I have to leave the office for a meeting in five minutes. You'll have to aggravate someone else for the rest of the day.

....

To: smills@alphamail.com
From: RoughRider16@bysmail.com

Let's have an email date tonight. I'll be home around nine. Meet me here then? Or we can IM if you'd rather?

....

BY 9:00 P.M., I'M not upset with RoughRider anymore. If anything, I've been counting down the minutes since Jack fell asleep while I was reading to him half an hour ago.

I thought about standing him up. He pretty much assumed in his message that I'd want to have an email date with him, and I didn't like that. Or maybe I just didn't like that he was right.

But then my afternoon meeting with some investors ran over, and I was on my way to meet Carmen and Jack for a late dinner at a pizza place when I got a call from Andrew Benson, the *Chicago Sun* reporter who wrote the article about Alpha Mail. He said he wants to write a follow-up, and I said of course. Then when I got to the pizza place, Jack was dressed as Darth Vader. As soon as I saw him, the last of my aggravation melted away. I told Carmen the good news about the follow-up article, and we were in high spirits all evening.

I'm really looking forward to my date with Mr. Anonymous when I sit down on my bed and open my laptop.

It's not something I could explain to anyone. I don't know who he is, but I feel like I can talk to him about anything. Maybe that's the appeal, though. I have nothing to lose because I don't know who he is.

Why doesn't he want me to know, though? That thought nags in the back of my mind. I'm wondering if RoughRider is just Ben trying to get to know me better in a playful way. If it's him . . . the thought gives me butterflies. If I have a real-life date with the man who has a knack for pissing me off and turning me on at the same time, well, that sounds *very* good.

I'm daydreaming about what Ben looks like under those suits of his when my email inbox updates with a new message.

....

To: smills@alphamail.com
From: RoughRider16@bysmail.com
Re: hey

How was your day?

....

To: RoughRider16@bysmail.com
From: smills@alphamail.com
Re: hey

It was good. Long meeting, great dinner. How about you?

....

To: smills@alphamail.com
From: RoughRider16@bysmail.com
Re: hey

Yeah, mine was good too. This is my busy season at work, and it's my favorite time.

I downloaded an IM app called Foxy. You have it?

....

To: RoughRider16@bysmail.com
From: smills@alphamail.com
Re: hey

It's installing right now . . . okay, done. I'm setting up my account . . . searching for your user name . . .

....

SIENNAM: *Hey, are you there?*

ROUGHRIDER16: *Yep. Thanks for downloading that. Should be easier to chat this way.*

SIENNAM: *So, mid-August is your busy season at work. Do you work at a heating and cooling place?*

ROUGHRIDER16: *My lips are sealed, remember?*

SIENNAM: *eyeroll*

ROUGHRIDER16: *wink*

SIENNAM: *Do you wink in real life?*

ROUGHRIDER16: *lol, not often, no. Why, you like it?*

SIENNAM: *I just admire a good winker is all. I'm a bad winker.*

ROUGHRIDER16: *A good winker? Am I the only one who thinks that sounds dirty?*

SIENNAM: *Yeah, I think you're reaching . . .*

ROUGHRIDER16: *Well, it rhymes with wanker. . . .*

SIENNAM: *Are you British?*

ROUGHRIDER16: *Nope.*

SIENNAM: *Tell me something about yourself.*

ROUGHRIDER16: *Okay . . . gimme a sec. . . .*

ROUGHRIDER16: *I beat a ninety-year-old at chess last weekend.*

SIENNAM: *Um, sweet? Did you flip over the table and scream "In your face!"?*

ROUGHRIDER16: *Nah. He was happier about it than I was. He's a chess wizard, used to teach it when he was younger. He lives in the same nursing home as my grandpa, and we've been playing chess every weekend for more than six months now. It was the first time I won.*

SIENNAM: *It doesn't sound so bad when you put it that way . . .*

ROUGHRIDER16: *lol, it wasn't bad at all. Dude's always busting my balls, saying things like, "You need to learn faster, son, or I'm gonna keel over before you ever win."*

SIENNAM: *He sounds like a fun guy.*

Rough Rider 16: *He is. He's one of my favorites.*

SIENNAM: *Now tell me something random from your childhood.*

ROUGHRIDER16: *From childhood? Damn, I don't know.*

SIENNAM: *Come on, just throw something out there.*

ROUGHRIDER16: *Okay, here's something that might make you smile. My dad sat me down for "the talk" when I was thirteen. He was more nervous than I was. I wanted to tell him I already knew the details, but I was afraid I'd get in trouble, so I stayed quiet. He broke out a pad and paper and talked for like an hour, complete with drawings of stick people to illustrate . . .*

SIENNAM: *OMG no! Stick people sex?*

ROUGHRIDER16: *Yep. It was brutal. If I ever have kids, there aren't gonna be any drawings when we have the talk . . .*

SIENNAM: *So you don't have kids—have you ever been married?*

ROUGHRIDER16: *No.*

SIENNAM: *Ever been close? Like, thought about it?*

ROUGHRIDER16: *No. It's your turn now. Tell me something about you.*

SIENNAM: *Okay . . . let me see . . . when I was finishing grad school, I seriously considered working for an organization that helps entrepreneurs in third-world countries start businesses. I would have traveled to new places to assist for a few months at a time. It was my dream job.*

ROUGHRIDER16: *Why didn't you do it?*

SIENNAM: *My best friend had gotten pregnant our senior year in college. The baby's father stayed with her at first, but then he left— didn't even tell her where he was going. She doesn't have family close by. She needed help with her son, so I stayed.*

ROUGHRIDER16: *That's admirable.*

SIENNAM: *Not really. I love her, and I love her son. He's the boy I mentioned, who's sick. I know if I would have been in that situation, she would have done the same for me.*

ROUGHRIDER16: *Have you ever thought about still doing that job someday?*

SIENNAM: *It would be hard now. I'm so involved in the day-to-day stuff at Alpha Mail. My goal is to open branches in two new cities within the next year, so then I'll travel between the three for a while.*

ROUGHRIDER16: *Are you happy with your work?*

SIENNAM: *Very.*

ROUGHRIDER16: *Now give me something random from your childhood. . . .*

SIENNAM: *Okay, this one's not as good without photographic evidence to support it, but when I was nine, I saw an actress on TV that I thought was really pretty, and I wanted to look like her. So I got some scissors and cut myself bangs, and since my mom wouldn't let me wear makeup, I used a blue marker as eyeshadow on my eyelids and a pink one as blush. When my mom got home and saw me, she started crying. The bangs were really awful. We laugh about it now. And of course, my brother breaks out the photos as often as he can.*

ROUGHRIDER16: *That's what brothers are for.*

SIENNAM: *I have a stash of photos of him with pimple cream and headgear, so there's that.*

ROUGHRIDER16: *I can tell you love him.*

SIENNAM: *I do. Very much. Do you have siblings?*

ROUGHRIDER16: *I have a little sister.*

SIENNAM: *So I've been doing some thinking. . . .*

ROUGHRIDER16: *Yeah . . .*

SIENNAM: *About your Bob/John situation . . .*

ROUGHRIDER16: *Okay. Tell me more.*

SIENNAM: *You said you feel like you have to give the promotion to Bob because he'll execute the job better.*

ROUGHRIDER16: *Unfortunately, yeah.*

SIENNAM: *Are you the boss at your job? The only one who gets to make this decision?*

RoughRider16: *Yes.*

SiennaM: *I think you should give it to John.*

RoughRider16: *I can understand that, and it's hard to explain, but . . . the results of the person in this position affect more than just him. Others won't be able to succeed in their roles if we don't have the best in the job Bob's getting.*

SiennaM: *Who is more senior at the company?*

RoughRider16: *John.*

SiennaM: *I feel even more strongly that he should get the job, then.*

RoughRider16: *Why?*

SiennaM: *You said he deserves it. He's worked hard. He has more heart. And as the boss, you get to decide what to reward in employees. Don't reward natural talent. Bob hasn't earned that job.*

SiennaM: *Hey, are you still here?*

RoughRider16: *Yes. I'm just thinking about what you said . . .*

SiennaM: *Sleep on it. See what you think tomorrow.*

RoughRider16: *I will.*

SiennaM: *I need to get to bed, but it was good to chat with you.*

RoughRider16: *It was. I like that you tell me what you really think, even if it's not what you think I want to hear.*

SiennaM: *Really? In that case, I think you're obnoxious for not telling me who you are.*

RoughRider16: *Goodnight, Sienna.*

SiennaM: *Goodnight.*

ELEVEN

#itskindacaveman

I'M ON MY second cup of coffee before nine the next morning. My mind is supposed to be on the office renovation plans the designer is going over with me, but instead, it's turning over my conversation with RoughRider from last night.

He said he has a sister but didn't mention a brother. If it was Ben, why wouldn't he mention his brother? To throw me off?

His exact words were "I have a little sister," which doesn't necessarily mean he doesn't *also* have a twin brother.

"Sienna?" Gretchen nudges me from her seat next to mine at the table in my office. "What do you think of that plan, to put the new logo on the floor in the lobby in stainless tile?"

"Oh." I look down at the designer's mock-up for the first time. "Looks great."

"And the text bubbles from the billboard campaign that we want to paint on the lobby walls?"

Gretchen turns to the next page in the design portfolio, and I scan the brightly colored text bubbles and the alpha messages they contain:

G'night, Gorgeous . . .

Love that sexy smile . . .
UR Mine

"Wait, no." I wrinkle my nose. "I don't know about the 'UR Mine' one. It's kinda caveman."

Gretchen smiles. "Yeah, but women love it."

I sip my coffee and mull. "Okay. You're the marketing manager, and it's up to you."

"Great." She gives me a triumphant smile.

"Do you guys need me for anything else?" I look at the two designers and then at Gretchen.

"No, we'll get out of your hair now."

Gretchen stands and leads the designers out of my office. She's good at reading my cues, and I was telling her I'm over looking at color swatches and paint chips. I'll let her handle those things.

I've got something else on my mind. It's an idea that came to me on my drive to the office this morning. I keep going back and forth on whether I should do it, though.

In theory, it's solid. Alpha Mail is technology-based. I have an IT team that works around the clock keeping our communications tech running smoothly. I invested in the top-of-the-line software and equipment they needed when I started the business. They can pinpoint anything I ask for—where my employees were when they sent a message to a client, what it said, what time the client read it, and even what sort of device they read it on.

If I want to know where RoughRider's messages are being sent from, my tech people can have an answer for me by the end of today.

And I do want to know—badly. Who is this man I've been chatting with every day? Is the intrigue I feel for him because of his anonymity, or is there really something there?

But what I *really* want is for him to tell me himself. If I find out who he is through my tech team, then what? It's not like I can tell him I went behind his back and dug up his identity against his wishes.

Maybe I don't want to know who he is. What if he doesn't want me to know for a good reason? He could be someone I can't be with for whatever reason, and then the intrigue would end. The messages would stop.

My gut is telling me to wait. RoughRider and I are slowly getting to know each other, and I haven't told him anything I'd be ashamed to have repeated. Every time I see a new message from him, I get a giddy sensation, and I don't want to do anything to mess with that.

I start returning emails, and I've almost worked my way through all the new ones when an instant message pops up on the screen of my phone. And of course, I smile, pick up the phone, and let myself get lost in my mystery man.

RoughRider16: *Good morning.*

SiennaM: *Good morning to you too.*

RoughRider16: *How's your day so far?*

SiennaM: *No complaints. How about you?*

RoughRider16: *It's a good day. I thought about our conversation last night when I was in the shower this morning, and you're right. I'm giving the promotion to John.*

SiennaM: *I'm glad to hear it. And you feel good about that decision, right?*

RoughRider16: *I do. I actually feel kind of shitty that I was going to give it to someone who doesn't deserve it for the wrong reasons.*

SIENNAM: *Windshields are bigger than rearview mirrors for a reason, you know. Look forward, not back.*

ROUGHRIDER16: *Okay, boss.*

SIENNAM: *Can I ask you a question?*

ROUGHRIDER16: *Of course.*

SIENNAM: *Why do alphas say "You are mine?" Like a woman needs to be constantly reminded or something? And like he owns her the same way he owns his car and his running shoes?*

ROUGHRIDER16: *Some guys say it because women like hearing it.*

SIENNAM: *Huh. Have you ever said it to a woman?*

ROUGHRIDER16: *No. I'm about actions rather than words, remember?*

SIENNAM: *So how do you show women they're yours?*

ROUGHRIDER16: *By never taking them for granted. Sending flowers, holding her hand when we're out, opening doors, remembering what's going on with her and asking about it, making her a part of my life . . . a woman who feels taken care of never doubts whose woman she is.*

SIENNAM: *Are you really an alpha?*

ROUGHRIDER16: *If you took one look at me, you'd know I am.*

SIENNAM: *Why? Are you big and imposing?*

ROUGHRIDER16: *You'd just know, trust me.*

SIENNAM: *So you never say things like, "You are mine?"*

ROUGHRIDER16: *I think you're secretly one of those women who likes it.*

SIENNAM: *I am not.*

ROUGHRIDER16: *Not even in bed?*

SIENNAM: *Is that when you like to say it?*

RoughRider 16: *I don't have a formula with women or anything. Like I said, it's been a while since I had a relationship, and to be honest, I've never had a very serious one.*

SIENNAM: *Never?*

ROUGHRIDER16: *Nope.*

SIENNAM: *By choice?*

ROUGHRIDER16: *lol, yeah, by choice. It's not that I can't find anyone who'd want me.*

SIENNAM: *What do you think is the first impression women get of you? That you're an alpha based on what they see, but what else? When they talk to you and start getting to know you?*

ROUGHRIDER16: *I think I come off quiet.*

SIENNAM: *But you aren't actually quiet?*

ROUGHRIDER16: *I am sometimes.*

SIENNAM: *Are you quiet in bed?*

ROUGHRIDER16: *Well, aren't you just full of questions today?*

SIENNAM: *You don't have to answer . . .*

ROUGHRIDER16: *I'd love to answer, as long as you'll reciprocate.*

SIENNAM: *I always reciprocate . . .*

ROUGHRIDER16: *Ugh, there you go getting me excited at work again . . .*

SIENNAM: *See that halo glowing above my head?*

RoughRider16: *Yeah, I see it all right . . . No, I'm not quiet in bed. If I'm ever guilty of being a stereotypical alpha, it's during sex.*

SiennaM: *Tell me you're going to tell me more . . . ?!*

RoughRider16: *I'd never want to disappoint you . . . so more it is. I'll never get to take you to bed, but if I could, that's when you'd see a side of me no one else ever sees. A side that's only for you. That's when I'd tell you how crazy you drive me in those skirts you wear and how much it turns me on hearing you say my name. You'd see me turn from the gentleman who makes you feel cherished every second of the day into a beast ruled only by his raging desire for you. I wouldn't leave an inch of you untouched or unsatisfied.*

SiennaM: *Not gonna lie, I'm liking the sound of that a lot.*

RoughRider16: *Yeah? My independent, take-no-shit girl wants to be subordinate in the bedroom?*

SiennaM: *Maybe . . . if it's to you.*

RoughRider16: *Fuck. Bad convo to have at work.*

SiennaM: *Yeah, I'm feeling flushed myself. Want me to change subjects?*

RoughRider16: *I'll reluctantly say yes . . .*

SiennaM: *Are you a commitment-phobe?*

RoughRider16: *No, I'd commit to the right woman.*

SiennaM: *I think I might be a commitment-phobe.*

RoughRider16: *Why?*

SiennaM: *The thought of a relationship unsettles me. I tried so many times, and every time, I was disappointed. It's just really hard/ impossible to find one person who does it for you in every way and have them feel the same in return. And then, things often fade in time.*

RoughRider16: *Not if you both work to not let it fade.*

SiennaM: *I guess so. It just seems idealistic to me.*

RoughRider16: *When's the last time you went on a date?*

SiennaM: *It's been a long time . . . close to a year. But I have one this weekend.*

RoughRider16: *Yeah? Who's the lucky guy?*

SiennaM: *Someone I met through work.*

RoughRider16: *Be careful.*

SiennaM: *About what? It's just a date?*

RoughRider16: *Just in general. Lots of guys aren't gentlemen.*

SiennaM: *Maybe you should take me out on a date, then . . .*

RoughRider16: *I wish I could.*

SiennaM: *Why can't you?*

RoughRider16: *I'm not avoiding, but I have to go. Work thing. Talk later?*

SiennaM: *Okay.*

TWELVE

#waitwhat

I'M EXCITED BUT not nervous about my date with Ben—until the moment he knocks on my door.

"You're sure I look okay?" I ask Carmen, smoothing down the front of my sleeveless green dress for at least the twentieth time.

"You look gorgeous." She gives me a reassuring smile, followed by a gentle shove toward the door. "Go open it."

When I open the door, I see Ben in something other than a suit for the first time. He looks good in jeans and a black polo, a few strands of his dark hair hanging down over his forehead.

"You look great," he says, his gaze sweeping down my body and back up again. "Ready to go?"

I nod and grab my bag, eager to get out of the house while Jack's still in the kitchen eating a snack. I don't want him getting any ideas about a man coming around here. The poor kid is starved for a man's attention, probably because his father is a deadbeat who hasn't seen him since he was two.

"How was your day?" Ben asks as we walk toward a sleek, dark sports car.

"Good. How about yours?"

He shrugs. "The usual. Gym and the office."

I feel his eyes on me as he opens the car door, and I fight back the familiar stab of annoyance it gives me. This isn't a guy just trying to get laid, it's someone I have an emotional connection with through our emails.

Maybe.

I study Ben's profile as he drives, trying to figure out how to prove or disprove my theory that he's my RoughRider.

"So . . ." I smile nervously.

He grins and looks over. "I'm glad you said yes to tonight. I've been wanting to go out with you since the first moment I saw you."

"We redheads have some fire, you know. Think you can handle it?"

"I know how to extinguish fire." He pats my knee.

I furrow my brow and look out the window. That comment was a far cry from RoughRider saying, "I love your fire. Never change." Then again, maybe that was a sexual reference—like he knows how to satisfy me.

God, I hope so. It's been a long time since any man has.

Our table at a trendy new restaurant called Trinity is secluded. We sit close together and share a bottle of white wine over dinner. Ben's full of entertaining stories about his job and life as an identical twin. He's also genuinely amused by my Alpha Mail stories.

"So I'm thinking dessert at my place," he says as he's signing the bill for dinner. "I got a white chocolate cheesecake I'm hoping you'll like."

I murmur a laugh, warm and buzzed from the alcohol and the flirting. "I'm sure I will."

Ben's hand starts out on my knee as he drives to his apartment, but it gradually moves higher. I really want to know if he's RoughRider before we go any further, but I don't want to spoil the moment. He'd tell me if he was ready, right?

So I stay quiet, enjoying the feel of his large, warm hand on my leg.

He leaves the car with the valet at his building, and I'm sure he's going to swallow me whole the moment we're on the elevator and no one else has gotten on, but he just eye-fucks me as we rise up to his floor. My heart races as I mentally undress him. The wine has me feeling very uninhibited.

His apartment is a penthouse with a lake view, though I can't see it well since it's nighttime. I'm gazing out the floor-to-ceiling windows in his living room, trying to imagine the expansive water scenery, when Ben wraps his arms around me from behind.

"I want to show you my bedroom," he says, his voice warm against my neck.

"Yes."

I want him, and in this moment, I don't even care if he's RoughRider. It's been so long since anyone has touched me this way—with affection and longing—and I don't want it to stop.

He leads the way into his bedroom, furnished in a minimal, modern style.

"I can get a little intense," he says softly as he bends down to kiss me.

"I'm good with intense," I murmur as his lips meet mine.

It's nice. I'm swimming in the sensations of warmth and excitement as he deepens the kiss.

"I want you so goddamn bad, Sienna." His voice is husky as he strips off his shirt.

His body is straight out of a men's fitness magazine. His chest is smooth and defined with muscle, and I run my fingers over it, getting a charge out of the feel of him.

"You sure you can handle what I want?" His eyes narrow as

he studies me while unbuttoning his pants.

"Yes." I can barely get the word out, my body humming with anticipation as he drops his pants and I take in his very respectable bulge.

I want to be taken by him. Ravaged until I'm not physically or emotionally hungry anymore. That will take time, but there's no other way I'd rather spend this night.

"Take your dress off," he says as he slides down his boxer briefs.

It's a little more perfunctory than I'd like, but whatevs. As long as we're both naked, we can get on to what I really want right now. I slide my dress up over my head, reveling in Ben's expression as I toss it to the floor.

"This is gonna be so good," he says.

His naked body is beyond impressive. Long, muscled legs, defined arms, and an erection standing at a ninety-degree angle to his body. When he grabs me and kisses me hard, I moan into his mouth. He's so warm against me, and I get lost in the feeling of wanting him.

Our hands explore, my body simmering under his touch. When he finally turns to the bed, I hum with satisfaction.

Ben climbs onto the white comforter of his bed, and I move to follow.

"Stay there," he says in a clipped tone.

I obey, liking that he knows what he wants. He gets on all fours on the mattress and turns his head to look back at me.

It's . . . not what I was expecting, but I smile automatically. Ben presses his cheek to the mattress then, his ass in the air as he speaks in a strangled tone.

"Spank my fucking ass, honey. As hard as you can. Set my ass on fire, please."

I freeze. Ben's clutching the comforter, his eyes begging me for the spanking.

"Um . . . I can do that."

I can, I tell myself. I'm a badass and a liberated woman. Since when do men always have to be in charge in the bedroom? Maybe Ben plans to reciprocate with a spanking of his own.

My arousal is running cold now, but I can get it back. Ben's got a body any woman would want to ride like a pony, for God's sake.

I approach him and clear my throat, pulling my hand back. I've never in my life spanked anyone.

Here goes nothing.

I almost laugh as my palm smacks against his skin. He groans with pleasure, so I stifle my amusement.

"Harder . . . please, harder," he mumbles.

I give him another slap, and then another. His sounds of pleasure are almost a whimper.

This is not what I was expecting. The thought keeps running through my head. I never would have thought this dark, physically big man would want me to spank him as foreplay. It's doing nothing for me, but since he's turned on . . . I suppose that's a good thing. I need him turned on so he can turn me on once again and satisfy me.

"Fuck yes," he says, pushing his ass back toward me. "Own me, Sienna. Tell me I'm a bad little bitch." He lifts his head and gives me a serious look. "You can finger-fuck my ass. I can take your whole hand."

I shake my head, looking at the floor and snatching up my dress as soon as I see it.

"I'm sorry, Ben, but I need to go."

He gets up to just his knees, his expression forlorn. "What? Why? We're just getting started."

"You're definitely not RoughRider," I mumble.

"Who?"

"I thought I didn't care." I shimmy into my dress. "I thought . . . a lot of things I shouldn't have thought. I'm sorry."

"Didn't care about what?"

"I'm gonna catch an Uber home." I grab my bag.

"Sienna . . . please don't go." Ben stands up, his tone pleading. "You're my fantasy. I've been dreaming about this since the day I saw you in your conference room. I need a strong, assertive woman to make my fantasies come true. And it's you."

I cringe inside. Why did I let myself get carried away by wine, my long sexual dry spell, and my feelings for RoughRider?

"It's not me," I say, putting my shoes on. "I'm sorry, Ben."

"You can use a dildo on my ass if you want," he offers. "I have a bunch."

I can't believe this is happening. One day, Carmen and I will laugh about this. But right now, I'm just mortified and I want out of here.

I shake my head and put a hand up to stop him as he rushes toward me.

"I'm leaving."

He sighs heavily as I practically break into a run on my way to the door. I don't take a deep breath until the elevator doors close behind me.

I'm feeling very sober now. And I'm also feeling irrationally pissed off at RoughRider. If I knew who he was, I wouldn't have ended up here with Ben, hoping he was the man I'm falling for.

I care, more than I even want to admit to myself. It's incredibly stupid to care this way for a man who doesn't want to reveal himself to me. Who may not be what he's made himself out to be. Tears flood my eyes, refusing to be held back.

When I step off the elevator, I put my head down, wipe my eyes, and head for the door to Ben's building.

I started this night wanting to be with RoughRider so badly, but right now, he's the last person in the world I want to talk to. I need a break from him. Possibly a permanent one.

THIRTEEN

#theforceisstrongwiththisone

WHEN CARMEN WALKS down the stairs, Jack and I inhale at the same time. The dark purple dress she picked for tonight is fitted on top, showing off her slender frame. The skirt flares out a little in that way that makes every woman feel like a princess.

"You're pretty, Mama," Jack says as she descends the last stair.

He's giving her a gap-toothed grin, eyes wide and shining with happiness. This might be the best idea I've ever had.

I'm feigning illness tonight, and as my best friend, I told Carmen she needed to do me a solid and go to the Firefighters' Ball with my brother.

I did it because she hasn't gotten dressed up for a night out in years, and I know this will be good for her. I can tell I was right by the way she's looking at herself in the mirror hanging above my couch.

"So this is what makeup is like," she murmurs. "I'd forgotten."

She runs her hand over her hair, which I styled in long, smooth waves. I love her for being so devoted to Jack that she doesn't worry about dating, makeup, or hair, but I also love that she's getting a night to be the beautiful woman she still is.

This is working out for both of us, because I'm not up for a night out. It's been a week since I spanked Ben and stopped messaging RoughRider. I'm finally feeling okay again, and I no longer think about reading the unopened messages from him on an hourly basis.

"Did you order the pizza, Cici?" Jack asks me.

I smile at his use of the nickname he hasn't used in a while. When he was a toddler, he couldn't pronounce "Sienna," so he started calling me "Cici."

"Yep. One extra large Giordano's with extra cheese."

"What movie are we watching?"

"You pick," I tell him, sitting down on the couch with a bag of chocolate-covered almonds.

"*Rogue One*. But we can't start it until the pizza gets here."

"Wanna play slapjack while we wait?"

Carmen interjects, a hand on her hip as she eyes us. "Sienna, you don't seem all that sick. This isn't a fix-up, is it?"

I arch my brows with surprise. "No, absolutely not. I'd never fix you up with Coop. He's a total player."

"What's a player?" Jack asks me.

"It's . . . someone who loves board games."

"Cool."

Carmen clears her throat. "You're not sick, though. What's this about?"

I give her a serious look and put a hand on my throat. "I told you, my throat hurts. I definitely need to take it easy tonight."

"Mmm-hmm." Her expression is skeptical.

"Just have fun, okay? Dance and drink and . . . be merry. All that good stuff."

She looks at her reflection in the mirror again. "I'll try."

When the doorbell rings, she jumps. I get up from the couch at the same time she turns to go open the door. She wobbles on one heel and then falls down, landing on her ass with a surprised squeal.

"I can't do this," she mutters. "Do you know how long it's been since I wore heels?"

"You're fine." I reach down to help her up. "Just lean on Coop all night. He's a sturdy guy."

She gives me a pleading look as she gets to her feet. "Promise me he doesn't think this is a date. I'm not up for a date."

"I swear, Carm. In fact, I told him he's in deep . . . excrement if he tries anything with you."

"What's extrement?" Jack asks.

"It's . . . yucky stuff." I wrinkle my nose and walk over to the front door, throwing it open.

Both Coop and the delivery guy from Giordano's are standing on the front porch.

"You buying me dinner?" I ask Coop with a grin.

"What the hell, may as well." He reaches for the wallet and passes the delivery guy several bills.

"Hey, thanks." The teenager arches his brows, apparently impressed with his tip.

I take the giant box, and Coop comes inside.

"Hey, you're looking pretty okay," I tell him, surveying him up and down.

He's wearing a tuxedo, his dark hair a perfect mix of messy and in place.

"Thanks. Can't say the same for you." He side-eyes my Pillsbury Doughboy pajama pants, which have the words "This Is How I Roll!" all over them. They're a perfect match for my baggy, threadbare Chicago Bears T-shirt.

"Jack's my date tonight, and he thinks I look amazing." I set the pizza box on the coffee table and flop down on the couch.

"Wow," Coop says softly.

I look between him and Carmen, my internal alarm sounding. I did not like the sound of that "wow." His eyes are wide as he keeps taking her in. She's blushing . . . blushing! I've never seen Carmen blush like she is right now.

Jack opens the box and reaches for a piece of pizza, oblivious to the visual foreplay happening just a few feet away.

"All right, you crazy kids!" I say, clapping my hands together. "Go enjoy your *completely platonic* evening together."

Coop tears his gaze away from Carmen and locks eyes with me, challenging me for just a second before he sees that I'm completely serious. I'm silently telling him—*again*—that I'll never forgive him if he messes with my best friend's emotions. She's fragile. He needs to find his one-night stands elsewhere. Carmen is my family.

His nod is almost imperceptible, but it tells me everything I need to hear. He's going to respect my wishes.

Coop reaches into his jacket pocket and takes out a small box. Carmen smiles when he opens it and takes out a tiny corsage of white flowers.

"Ha! I get your corsage now," she says to me with a grin.

"I picked this out just for you," Coop says as he slides it onto her wrist. "Got it on my way here, and I already knew you were my date."

Carmen's smile slides away, and the blush returns. "It's so pretty. Thank you."

"I want to see, Mama." Jack gets off the couch and bounces over to admire the flowers.

"What's this in my other pocket?" Coop looks confused as he reaches in and pulls out something shiny. "Ah, that's right. This is for you, Jack."

Jack's mouth drops open when he sees the shiny gold

firefighter's badge. "For me?"

"Yep." Coop gets down on one knee to pin it onto Jack's Darth Vader pajama top. "A bunch of the guys saw you in action when you came to the station for that tour. Your siren-blaring and hose-holding skills were the best we've ever seen in a kid your age. We want you to be an honorary firefighter."

Jack grins and looks up at Carmen. "It has my name on it, look!" He runs his finger over the letters on the badge.

I have to close my eyes to hold back the tears clouding my vision. Flawed as Cooper Mills may be, I love him fiercely, and this is why.

"Let me grab a picture of you two real quick," I say, clearing my throat to get rid of the lump there.

Coop stays on one knee, and Jack puts an arm around his neck. Their smiles make me tear up again. If only things were different. If only there were even a chance Jack could beat the horrible disease he has.

I try to live in the now and feel the joy, but bitter anger starts to creep in. It's so unfair that this beautiful boy, so full of light and happiness, will never reach adulthood.

"Take one of me and Mom too," Jack says.

Carmen smiles brightly for the photo, giving me the mental reset I needed. If she can be in the now, so can I.

"I can keep this, right?" Jack asks Coop.

"Absolutely. But if you do, it means you have to come by the station to have dinner with us sometimes. Make sure you're wearing your badge so everyone knows you're one of us."

Jack nods eagerly. I meet Coop's gaze with a grateful look.

"Ready?" He offers Carmen his arm, and she takes it.

I get up to close the door behind them and lock it, and then I settle in on the couch with Jack for pizza, *Star Wars*, and snuggles.

It's the first time since I stopped communicating with RoughRider that I feel completely content.

THE SOUND OF the front door opening makes me stir. I can barely make out Carmen's outline in the dusky light.

I fell asleep curled up in a chair in the living room, and my neck aches when I move to get up. Instinctively, I look over at Jack, who's snoring on the couch, to confirm he's okay.

"Hey," I whisper to Carmen. "What time is it?"

"Uh . . . four thirty." She's holding her heels in her hand and tiptoeing over to the stairway.

"A.m.?" I whisper-shout.

"Yeah. I'm going to bed."

I walk over to her as quietly, yet quickly, as I can, my heart pounding. "What did he do? Did you guys sleep together?"

She looks down. "No."

"If you did, tell me."

Carmen tips her face up to meet my gaze. "We didn't. He never laid a hand on me. We went to the ball, and it was great. Then we went to a diner to eat, and after that, we just walked around and talked."

"Until 4:30 a.m.?" I narrow my eyes skeptically.

"Yes, Mom. Now let me get some sleep before Jack wakes up."

I wave dismissively. "I'll take him out for breakfast and the park or something. Sleep late."

"Thanks." She turns to walk upstairs.

"Why do you look sad?"

Carmen sighs and doesn't turn around. "Can we not talk about it right now?"

"I guess so . . . but I'm gonna call my brother and ask him what he did if you don't tell me."

She turns to face me. "He didn't do anything. Just—" she puts a hand up "—back off for now, please?"

"Okay. But I'm here if you need me. Don't feel like you can't bitch about Coop to me because he's my brother."

She gives me a half smile before turning away and walking upstairs. I go back to my chair, where I can keep an eye on Jack, and after an hour of restlessness, I finally fall back asleep.

MUCH LATER THAT morning, Jack and I are walking back from eating at a restaurant a couple blocks from home when we pass some kids playing in a small, fenced-in yard. Jack gives them a longing look, which tugs at my heart.

He played with kids at the park for more than an hour before we left there to go eat breakfast, but I know it's not the same. The kids in the yard are laughing and are clearly familiar with each other. Jack went to kindergarten last year and will attend first grade starting soon, and he misses his friends.

"Are you all set for school to start?" I ask him.

"Yeah."

"You guys got all your supplies and stuff, right?"

He nods. "All I need is new underwear."

"You want some princess underwear?"

He laughs and wrinkles his nose. "No, Cici . . . I want *Star Wars*. They didn't have that kind at the store Mom took me to."

"Ah. I wish I could have some *Star Wars* underwear."

Jack laughs louder this time. "They don't make *Star Wars* underwear for grown-ups."

"I know." I sigh heavily. "I wish they did, though. I'd want Han Solo on mine."

"And Luke Skywalker?"

"Definitely him too. And Jabba the Hut."

"Not him!" Jack giggles and gives me a look that tells me he thinks I've lost it.

"No? You don't like him?"

"He's a bad guy."

"True. I guess I wouldn't want bad guys on my drawers. Bad mojo and all."

"You're funny."

I grin down at him and take his hand to cross the final intersection before home. When I look ahead at our block, I see a cluster of people out in the street. I squint and see that many of them are dressed in white.

"Something's going on up there," I murmur.

Keeping Jack's hand in mine, I watch the group, and my heart pounds a little as we get closer. The people wearing white are dressed as Stormtroopers from the movie *Star Wars*—and there are a couple dozen of them.

"What's going on?" Jack asks, looking up at me.

"I don't know, sweets."

When we're almost back to the brownstone, someone in the group seems to recognize Jack, because the Stormtroopers move into formation in the middle of the street, which is closed to traffic. And just when I think it can't get any more surreal, Darth Vader takes his place in front of the group and the song "Uptown Funk" starts to play.

It seems to be some sort of flash mob, and Jack is beside himself with excitement. Carmen is sitting on the front steps, grinning from ear to ear, and Jack runs to sit in her lap and watch the performance.

They're good, and the image of Darth Vader dancing and swinging his light saber to the song is too funny not to laugh at. The Stormtroopers all keep pace behind him. Neighbors are standing outside watching the performance, all of them smiling.

I take out my phone to record the rest of the dance, also getting footage of Jack in Carmen's lap, both of them obviously delighted. She rests her head on his, looking joyful and blissfully unaware she's wearing pajama pants, a T-shirt, and a messy bun.

When the song ends, the Stormtroopers all stand in perfect formation, and Darth Vader approaches Jack.

"Jack Elliott?" he asks, his voice a deep, authentically filtered version of the real Darth's.

"Yes, sir." Jack looks up at him, his eyes wide and awestruck.

I realize that in his little mind, this is *the* Darth Vader, and it melts me.

"Your father sent me," Darth says. "He loves you very much and said you've got the heart of a Jedi."

"My dad? You know my dad?" Jack's smile is wide.

"Yes. Remember that the Jedi are always with you in your heart. Will you do that?"

Jack nods and Darth touches the top of his head before standing, giving a flick of his hand to the assembled Stormtroopers and leading them down the street. The neighbors who were watching clap and cheer as the Stormtroopers slow-jog in formation.

Neighbor kids approach the front steps, all of them wowed by what just happened and dying to know how Jack knows Darth Vader.

Carmen lets him enjoy being swarmed, and she walks over to me with an incredulous look.

"Did you do that?" she asks me in a whisper.

"No."

"I haven't heard a peep from Danny in almost four years . . ." Her voice is nearly inaudible so no one but me can hear. "Do you really think he could have . . . ?"

"It sounds like it."

She smiles, her expression softening. "Jack's going to have some great stories when school starts, between that fireman's badge and this."

I hug her and hold up the brown paper bag in my hand. "We brought you some of those banana walnut pancakes you like."

"You're amazing."

"So are you."

She furrows her brow. "Do you think maybe . . . Coop did that?"

"One way to find out." I take out my phone and press the button to call my brother.

After a few rings, he answers in a pissy, sleepy tone. "We didn't do anything, I swear. We walked and talked, that's it."

"I know. I was just wondering if you set up the flash mob that just happened in front of my house."

"Flash mob?" he asks, irritated. "I had to stop by the station after I dropped Carmen off, and I've only been asleep for an hour. Are you fucking with me right now?"

"No. Go back to sleep. Sorry I woke you up."

He grunts and hangs up.

"Wasn't him," I tell Carmen. "So I guess Danny did set it up."

Carmen wraps her arms around herself and smiles. "For all he's done wrong, and there's plenty . . . that meant everything to Jack."

We walk inside, and Carmen lets Jack talk to the neighborhood kids alone on the porch. She keeps watch the entire time from the front window, of course. But still, it's the most normal moment he's ever had with the neighbor kids, and that means as much to me as it does to Carmen.

FOURTEEN

THE CURSOR ON my office computer screen flashes, daring me to hit "Send" this time. Or maybe not, but I need the nudge, so I interpret it that way and click the button before I can overthink it.

I've written this message twice now, deleted it, and rewritten it. The third time's apparently a charm.

....

To: RoughRider16@bysmail.com
From: smills@alphamail.com
Re: hi again

Hi. Apparently, I don't know how to quit you. You're like a drinking habit, only I don't even get a buzz.

S

....

I start working my way through my jammed Monday-morning email inbox. There's a message from the Alpha Mail attorney with good news about the property I'm trying to acquire for a New York office, word from a detective at the Chicago Police Department that an order of protection has been approved for Isaac against his crazed client, and an email from Ben that I can't bring myself to read. No matter what he has to say, I'll never be able to look him in the eye again without thinking about him asking me to put my entire hand up his ass.

When a response from RoughRider appears, though, I pounce on it.

....

To: smills@alphamail.com
From: RoughRider16@bysmail.com
Re: about fucking time

Where have you been? Have you not seen the dozen plus messages I've sent you? And now you're back after more than a week and pissed off at me? Should be the other way around. I was worried about you.

....

To: RoughRider16@bysmail.com
From: smills@alphamail.com
Re: about fucking time

Do you think you should be the one making the rules all the time? I've been busy, and I was cooling off, because you weren't my favorite person for a while. You still aren't, tbh . . .

....

To: smills@alphamail.com
From: RoughRider16@bysmail.com
Re: about fucking time

Oh, yeah? Back at ya. Last I knew, you were going out with some guy. I've been wondering if you were dead in a ditch somewhere or shacked up in bed with him in Vegas or something. And back and forth on which I'd prefer.

....

To: RoughRider16@bysmail.com
From: smills@alphamail.com
Re: about fucking time

Really????? I mean . . . REALLY? You were frustrated because you didn't know where I was, when you could have picked up the phone to call me and ask? Imagine how it feels to be frustrated because I don't know WHO YOU ARE. Also, fuck you.

....

To: smills@alphamail.com
From: RoughRider16@bysmail.com
Re: about fucking time

That's a fair criticism. I'm sorry for jumping all over you, and I shouldn't have made that comment about not being sure which I'd prefer. I'm sorry for that too. So you're right—fuck me. Forgive me?

....

To: RoughRider16@bysmail.com
From: smills@alphamail.com
Re: about fucking time

I guess so. I'm still pissed off that I missed you, though, and I'm not getting over that until I'm good and ready.

....

To: smills@alphamail.com
From: RoughRider16@bysmail.com
Re: about fucking time

You missed me? I missed you too. More than you know.

Have you been seeing the guy you went out with?

....

To: RoughRider16@bysmail.com
From: smills@alphamail.com
Re: about fucking time

No. I actually thought the guy I was going out with might be you. But then I found out he wasn't, and it was disappointing and awful. I was upset. That's why I stopped messaging you.

....

To: smills@alphamail.com
From: RoughRider16@bysmail.com
Re: about fucking time

I'm sorry, Sienna. That makes me feel like shit. I never should have messaged you in the first place. You're the last person in the world I'd ever want to hurt.

....

To: RoughRider16@bysmail.com
From: smills@alphamail.com
Re: about fucking time

You wish you'd never messaged me? Do you think we should stop?

....

To: smills@alphamail.com
From: RoughRider16@bysmail.com
Re: about fucking time

No. I can never have you the way I want to, but if this is as close as I can get, I'll take it.

....

To: RoughRider16@bysmail.com
From: smills@alphamail.com
Re: about fucking time

Will you at least tell me why you can't have me? Give me something.

....

To: smills@alphamail.com
From: RoughRider16@bysmail.com
Re: about fucking time

I can't. Telling you that would reveal who I am. Please understand.

....

To: RoughRider16@bysmail.com
From: smills@alphamail.com
Re: about fucking time

I wish I could, but if knowing would ruin things between us, what we're doing is probably wrong on some level. You said you aren't married, but are you separated or in a complicated relationship? I can't handle being part of something like that.

....

To: smills@alphamail.com
From: RoughRider16@bysmail.com
Re: about fucking time

No—I'm not involved with any woman in any way. It's nothing like that.

I'm relieved it didn't work out with that guy. I was so jealous over that I couldn't see straight.

....

To: RoughRider16@bysmail.com
From: smills@alphamail.com
Re: about fucking time

Is that so? I thought true alphas didn't get jealous and pos-sessive . . .

....

To: smills@alphamail.com
From: RoughRider16@bysmail.com
Re: about fucking time

I wouldn't be if we were together. But I'm just here fucking helpless, not knowing what's going on. He didn't do anything to you, did he?

....

To: RoughRider16@bysmail.com
From: smills@alphamail.com
Re: about fucking time

What, something bad? No, nothing like that.

....

To: smills@alphamail.com
From: RoughRider16@bysmail.com
Re: about fucking time

Did you fuck him?

....

To: RoughRider16@bysmail.com

From: smills@alphamail.com
Re: about fucking time

Excuse me? Like that's any of your business, random person whose identity I don't even know?

....

To: smills@alphamail.com
From: RoughRider16@bysmail.com
Re: about fucking time

Tell me. Did you?

....

To: RoughRider16@bysmail.com
From: smills@alphamail.com
Re: about fucking time

So when I want you to tell me who you are, you brush me off, but I owe you explanations about the intimate details of my sex life?

....

To: smills@alphamail.com
From: RoughRider16@bysmail.com
Re: about fucking time

TELL. ME.

....

To: RoughRider16@bysmail.com
From: smills@alphamail.com
Re: about fucking time

No, I didn't "fuck him," Casanova.

....

To: smills@alphamail.com
From: RoughRider16@bysmail.com
Re: about fucking time

Why sugarcoat it? That's all it would have been with someone you don't love.

....

To: RoughRider16@bysmail.com
From: smills@alphamail.com
Re: about fucking time

And what's wrong with that? You think two single, consenting adults can't have sex just for fun?

....

To: smills@alphamail.com
From: RoughRider16@bysmail.com
Re: about fucking time

Sure they can, but that's not for me, and I don't think it's for you either.

....

To: RoughRider16@bysmail.com
From: smills@alphamail.com
Re: about fucking time

I don't even know what's for me anymore. I do know life was easier when I was closed off to all men, even anonymous ones.

....

To: smills@alphamail.com
From: RoughRider16@bysmail.com

Re: about fucking time

Easier isn't necessarily better. I hate to do this, but I have to sign off for a work thing. IM date tonight?

....

To: smills@alphamail.com
From: RoughRider16@bysmail.com
Re: about fucking time

Okay.

....

WHEN I WALK into the break room after my message exchange with RoughRider, Isaac and Kell are sitting at a table eating sandwiches.

"Hey, how's it going?" I ask as I walk over to the stainless steel refrigerator and open it to grab a bottle of water.

"Eh." Kell grunts and shrugs.

"Good talk," I say with a wry smile.

He gives me the playboy grin that keeps his client roster full. "Sorry. I just got an ass-chewing from a pissed-off husband."

"Oh, you mean . . . his wife is a client?"

"Yep."

"Tell him to take it up with her."

"Oh, I did. But the douchebag still wouldn't quit. Called me every name under the sun and accused me of giving his wife unrealistic expectations about men."

I sit down at the round table. "You don't have to put up with that, Kell."

"She's on the unlimited plan, and he was texting me from her phone, so . . . I kinda did."

"No, I don't want you guys dealing with that stuff. I'll talk to the attorney about drawing up a new policy so this doesn't happen again."

"Thanks." He brushes the crumbs from his hands and stands up. "Good sandwiches, by the way."

"I think Jane switched caterers."

"Yeah." He glances at his watch. "Duty calls."

I chat briefly with Isaac, who tells me he's relieved he got a restraining order against his stalker client. Poor guy, he seems genuinely fearful of the woman who had his name tattooed on her. I can see why—she sounds completely unbalanced.

Before leaving the break room, I grab a sandwich from the fridge. I'm walking back to my office, food and drink in hand, when the sound of a deep, growly male voice makes me slow down.

"Fuck, baby. You've got me so hard for you right now. Tug on those nipples for me . . . yeah. Squeeze them hard like you know I would."

My slow walk turns into a complete stop. The voice I'm mesmerized by is Dane's. Apparently, he's not as grumpy with clients as he is with me.

"Yeah, my hand is wrapped all the way around my cock. It's so fucking hard. You want me to go slow or fast?"

My brows arch involuntarily, and I grip the bottle of water in my hand. I'm the boss here, and this is just another way of keeping up with what's going on with my employees, no different from talking to Isaac and Kell in the break room just now.

Right . . . but talking to Isaac and Kell didn't turn me on. I'm not sure if that's a job perk or a job hazard, but I do know one thing—I'm staying outside this door, out of Dane's sight but well within reach of his gravelly voice.

"You're soaked, aren't you, baby?" he croons. "Slide those fingers inside for me. Tell me how it feels."

I close my eyes, thinking of RoughRider. Maybe I can convince him to let me hear his voice. I think if he and I could have conversations like this, I could make do with not being with him in person.

"Faster," Dane coaxes. "I have to go faster, babe. The thought of you lying there with your legs spread, fingering that gorgeous pussy is just too much for me . . . oh, shit . . . feels so good . . ."

I should probably tell him to close his door . . . but not now. Later. I'll tell him later.

For now, I'm riveted, straining to hear Dane's next words. He's right, it *does* feel good, in places that shouldn't feel good at work.

Gretchen is approaching me, her mouth open like she's about to say something. I put a finger to my lips and motion for her to stand next to me by the wall.

"Fuuuuuck, baby." Dane groans loudly, and Gretchen's eyes widen with surprise. "Come hard for me. Oh, shit . . . yeah, I did. I shot a huge load off thinking of you."

Gretchen and I exchange a look that's half curious and half concerned. I can't help myself—I poke my head around the doorway to look at Dane.

He's sitting at his desk, fully clothed, working on a Rubik's Cube as he talks into the headset he's wearing.

"Yeah, baby. Lick it all off your fingers for me. You know how I like that."

When he sees me, he raises his hand in a friendly wave, like he's talking about the weather right now or something. I smile awkwardly, weirded out knowing I was aroused by his fake arousal.

"Okay, babe . . . me too. Have a great day."

He presses a button to disconnect the call and then takes off his headset.

"Hey, you need me for something?"

Yes. *God*, yes. I need him for all the things I just heard him talking about. He may not have been into it, but I sure as hell was. Am I just undersexed, or is Dane as hot as I'm thinking he is right now?

"Uh . . . no. I just overheard you and wanted to say, you know, great job."

"Heh." He reaches a hand around the back of his neck. "Thanks."

"So . . . you're happy here, right?"

He nods. "Yeah, I'm good, why?"

"I just want you to be happy so you'll stay. You're good at this job."

"I'm planning on staying till I finish school."

"Okay, good."

"Hey, thanks for replacing the coffeemaker."

Sure thing. Thanks for almost getting me off as I walked past your office.

I wave a hand, dismissing his thanks. "No problem."

"Did you need anything else?" He gives me an impatient look. "I've got another client."

Ah, there's the brooding grouch I'm used to.

"Nope, just . . . carry on."

I turn to find Gretchen, but she's gone. I'm okay with that. Right now, I just want to be alone in my office so I can think about what I just overheard.

I can't wait for my IM date with RoughRider tonight. I hope I can talk him into a phone call. Hearing Dane talking to that client made me realize that while I really like reading RoughRider's words, him saying them to me would be even better. And if that voice happens to be Dane's . . . well, I wouldn't be disappointed. Company policy be damned.

FIFTEEN

#IMhorny

ROUGHRIDER16: *Hey, how are you?*

SIENNAM: *Not bad. You?*

ROUGHRIDER16: *I have the attention of a beautiful woman. Never been better.*

SIENNAM: *Do you like coffee?*

ROUGHRIDER16: *No. I mostly drink water. Why?*

SIENNAM: *Just curious.*

ROUGHRIDER16: *You know what I do like?*

SIENNAM: *???*

ROUGHRIDER16: *The thought of silencing that sharp tongue of yours with a kiss.*

SIENNAM: *Sharp, hmm?*

ROUGHRIDER16: *Don't worry, I know it's mostly just your sexual frustration talking when you're salty.*

SiennaM: *Hang on . . .*

SiennaM: *Sorry, just another sec . . .*

SiennaM: *Okay, I'm back. I was laughing really hard there for a minute. What the hell would you know about my sexual frustration?*

RoughRider16: *I know I could turn that roar of yours into a purr.*

SiennaM: *Do tell, O Rough one . . .*

RoughRider16: *I'd start with a massage. Slowly and sensually caressing every inch of you, but not the places you really want me to touch. I'd just suffer the sounds of your moans and the arch of your back as you silently begged me for more.*

SiennaM: *That does sound like a strong start . . .*

RoughRider16: *Then I'd repeat the process with my mouth.*

SiennaM: *You would.*

SiennaM: *I mean . . . you would? cringe of embarrassment*

RoughRider16: *grin*

RoughRider16: *Never be embarrassed around me.*

SiennaM: *What would you do next?*

RoughRider16: *Kiss you. Hard and fast. Slow and soft. I'd kiss you until your lips were tingling and your chest was rising and falling as you panted my name.*

SiennaM: *I'd kiss you back. I'd wind my hand into your hair, close my eyes, and just inhale you. Even if I couldn't see you, just knowing what you feel and sound and taste like would be . . . more. It would be everything, really. The whole world knows what you look like.*

RoughRider16: *Wow. I'm very turned on right now.*

SIENNAM: *Me too.*

ROUGHRIDER16: *Was your first time having sex a good experience?*

SIENNAM: *I think it was better than most. It was with a high school boyfriend. We were both 17. He was patient and gentle. What about you?*

ROUGHRIDER16: *Well, I'm a guy. I think our first time is always a good experience.*

SIENNAM: *Why don't I get any details?*

ROUGHRIDER16: *I'll tell you whatever you want to know. I was 16, she was 18. She lived in my neighborhood.*

SIENNAM: *Was she a virgin too?*

ROUGHRIDER16: *Yeah.*

SIENNAM: *Was it a one-time only thing?*

ROUGHRIDER16: *No, it was a few times.*

SIENNAM: *You must've been good.*

ROUGHRIDER16: *Back then, who knows. I hope I was.*

SIENNAM: *But now you know you're good?*

ROUGHRIDER16: *I've gotten excellent feedback.*

SIENNAM: *But were they telling the truth?*

ROUGHRIDER16: *I assume so. But I can feel it when a woman comes, so I'd know if they were lying.*

SIENNAM: *What sorcery is this?*

ROUGHRIDER16: *A man just has to pay attention. If he's not completely focused on his own dick, it's pretty obvious . . .*

SIENNAM: *How so?*

ROUGHRIDER16: *You really want to know all this?*

SIENNAM: *I really do. Whisper your pussy expertise.*

ROUGHRIDER16: *Well, if I were inside you, here's how I'd know you were coming . . . you'd clench around me really tight, and I'd feel you start to spasm. It would take all my self-control to hold on and not let that squeezing sensation milk me dry.*

SIENNAM: *Um . . . that sounds nice. You can feel that?*

ROUGHRIDER16: *Yep.*

SIENNAM: *What turns you on?*

ROUGHRIDER16: *Right now? Thoughts of you. What your hair would feel like on my chest, how your nipples taste, what you wear to bed, that kind of thing. What about you?*

SIENNAM: *Well . . . this.*

ROUGHRIDER16: *You like dirty talk?*

SIENNAM: *Sometimes. Most men aren't very good at it. They just repeat the same two or three things over and over again . . .*

ROUGHRIDER16: *You'd look like a goddess on top of me, you know. With that red hair down your arched back and your hips grinding against me. I wouldn't be able to let you ride me for long.*

SIENNAM: *Because you'd come?*

ROUGHRIDER16: *Hell no. Because I'd grab your hips and pound you fucking senseless.*

SIENNAM: *Oh. I think I'd like that.*

ROUGHRIDER16: *You think?*

SIENNAM: *This is frustrating. I want you.*

ROUGHRIDER16: *I want you back.*

SIENNAM: *I'm all wet and completely alone. So sad.*

ROUGHRIDER16: *FUCKING HELL. You're making me crazy.*

SIENNAM: *You gonna do something about it?*

ROUGHRIDER16: *Why don't you do something for me? Slip your hand into your panties.*

SIENNAM: *I want to, but . . . I can't.*

ROUGHRIDER16: *Why not?*

SIENNAM: *Because I don't know who you are, and . . . I'm just not there yet.*

ROUGHRIDER16: *I understand. And I'm glad you were honest with me.*

SIENNAM: *I will be going to bed very hot and bothered, though.*

ROUGHRIDER16: *Me too.*

SIENNAM: *So tired, but talk again soon?*

ROUGHRIDER16: *Yes. Sweet dreams, Sienna. Or maybe not so sweet . . . ?*

SIENNAM: *I'll never tell.*

SIXTEEN

#stalkersgonnastalk

ROUGHRIDER HAS NEVER touched me, but *damn*, is he under my skin. Our IM dates have become a nightly thing. When I got out of the shower yesterday evening, thinking of messaging him for our date, I already had a message from him.

> ROUGHRIDER16: *Sorry, something urgent came up. I'll be tied up for a while. I'll msg tomorrow.*

I'd been disappointed, which would have been funny if it hadn't been so sad. How could I have let myself get so wrapped up in someone I don't really know anything about?

My heels click on the concrete floor of the office hallway a little louder than necessary. I'm crabby and eager to wrap my hands around the cup of Starbucks Jane always has waiting for me.

But when I look at Jane's desk, it's not my coffee that grabs my attention. Ben Durant is leaning against the wall, apparently chatting with my assistant.

"Sienna." He stands up straight when he sees me. "Why haven't you returned my messages?"

Ugh. I made a big mistake going out with an investor. Now I have to figure out how to untangle myself from this mess.

"I've just been really busy."

His expression is skeptical and contrite at the same time. "Can we talk in your office?"

In my mind, I'm replaying this tall, seemingly average man begging me to tell him he's a bad little bitch. And not only do I not want to think about that night ever again, I definitely don't want to talk about it.

"I . . . might be able to do that." I look at Jane, trying to telegraph my desperation. "How's my schedule this morning?"

"Wide open." She grins victoriously.

Shit, shit, shit.

"Come on in," I tell Ben.

Jane and I need to work on some nonverbal signals for future reference. She's still looking pleased with herself when she calls out, "Oh, delivery for you on your desk, Sienna. I left your coffee there too."

"Thanks," I say weakly.

The delivery turns out to be an enormous bouquet of red flowers. There are a half-dozen different blooms, all the same gorgeous shade, arranged in a tall, cut glass vase.

"Oh, Ben." My shoulders drop, and I look at him. "You shouldn't have."

He arches his brows with surprise. "I didn't."

"They're not from you?"

"No. I wish they were, though."

Furrowing my brow, I walk over to the flowers, their sweet scent greeting me as I pluck a small white envelope from its holder.

When I read it, my pulse quickens.

I'm sorry about last night. I know the ride's been rough lately, but you still mean everything to me.

RoughRider sent me these flowers. That's very real. This is the first tangible sign of the man whose identity eludes me. I do matter to him.

"Are you seeing someone else?" Ben asks, his tone hurt.

Thinking fast, I realize this is my out.

"Yes. We've had a long-term thing, actually, and we were on a break when I went out with you, but we're back together now."

"Back together?" He looks deflated. "So there's no chance for us?"

No chance in hell, I want to say. *You'll have to find someone else to spank you and fist your ass.*

"I'm sorry," I say instead. "I didn't mean to lead you on."

Ben sighs softly and looks at the floor. "Okay. Can we keep what happened between us private?"

Ha! As if I'd ever want anyone to know about it.

"Absolutely. Thank you for understanding."

He leaves my office looking dejected, and I exhale deeply. Bullet dodged.

I admire the flowers and read the card again before sitting down to message RoughRider, unable to keep the silly smile from my face.

SIENNAM: *The flowers are gorgeous. Thank you.*

He writes back immediately.

ROUGHRIDER16: *Good. I chose red for your hair. It's beautiful.*

SIENNAM: *Thank you. Will you tell me what color your hair is?*

ROUGHRIDER16: *It's dark.*

SIENNAM: *I have something to confess.*

ROUGHRIDER16: *Lord, woman, we just made up ten seconds ago. Lol, let's hear it.*

SIENNAM: *I thought about having my IT department figure out who you are.*

SIENNAM: *. . . ? Are you still there?*

ROUGHRIDER16: *Yeah, I'm here. You thought about it, but didn't?*

SIENNAM: *No. It didn't feel right.*

ROUGHRIDER16: *They wouldn't have been able to find me anyway. I took precautions.*

SIENNAM: *That sounds ominous . . .*

ROUGHRIDER16: *It's not. I just figured curiosity would get the better of you, so I got untraceable accounts.*

SIENNAM: *Nothing's untraceable.*

ROUGHRIDER16: *True. But these would trace to someone other than me.*

SIENNAM: *You're never going to tell me who you are, are you?*

ROUGHRIDER16: *Can't we just enjoy what we have?*

SIENNAM: *Don't you want more than this?*

ROUGHRIDER16: *Of course, but this is better than nothing.*

SIENNAM: *I'd love to hear your voice.*

ROUGHRIDER16: *Maybe at some point.*

SIENNAM: *Tell me something about you. Anything.*

ROUGHRIDER16: *I'm dog-sitting a friend's German Shepherd for a week, and I don't want to give him back. Best damn dog I've ever been around.*

SIENNAM: *What's his name?*

ROUGHRIDER16: *Samson*

SIENNAM: *Do you have any pets?*

ROUGHRIDER16: *No, it wouldn't be fair with my schedule. I want a dog someday, though.*

SIENNAM: *What are you wearing right now?*

ROUGHRIDER16: *khakis and a polo . . . you?*

SIENNAM: *black skirt and blue shirt*

ROUGHRIDER16: *a skirt . . . something to fantasize about all day . . .*

SIENNAM: *Skirts do it for you, huh?*

ROUGHRIDER16: *Yes, if you're wearing them.*

SIENNAM: *What's your favorite kind of ice cream?*

ROUGHRIDER16: *Strawberry. Yours?*

SIENNAM: *Cookies and cream.*

ROUGHRIDER16: *If you could go anywhere in the world for a vacation, where would you choose?*

SIENNAM: *Hmm . . . an island, I think. Somewhere with a beach and fruity drinks. You?*

ROUGHRIDER16: *I'd go anywhere with you. Antarctica. Siberia. Alcatraz . . . those all sound fun if you'd be there with me.*

SIENNAM: *Let's stick with me choosing destinations . . .*

ROUGHRIDER16: *Deal. Hey, I have to do some work. I'll msg later today.*

SIENNAM: *Okay.*

ROUGHRIDER16: *I meant what I said on the card.*

SIENNAM: *xoxo*

I sign off the IM app and turn my attention to work. I'm making decent progress, but I can't help looking at the flowers and card on my desk every now and then. Each time, I feel warm inside.

Is it crazy to be falling so hard for someone I don't even know? Maybe, but I can't help myself. Besides, I *do* know him. Like he said, we've met, I just don't know which of my male acquaintances he is.

I realize I've got it bad when I walk to a nearby deli to pick up lunch, bringing the carryout order back to my office rather than eating there because I don't want to miss RoughRider's next message by being gone too long.

The independent, no-fucks-given woman I was a month ago is turning into a mushy mess over this guy. But for once, instead of considering all the potential pitfalls, I'm just enjoying it. It feels too good to do anything else.

It's midafternoon by the time I get a new message from him, and my heart rate kicks up a notch when I do.

ROUGHRIDER16: *Hey, how's your day going?*

SIENNAM: *Good. Productive. How's yours?*

ROUGHRIDER16: *It's good. A little crazy, but good.*

SIENNAM: *Where did you say you work?*

ROUGHRIDER16: *I work in a building.*

SIENNAM: *Cute. eyeroll*

ROUGHRIDER16: *wink*

SIENNAM: *So I'm doing a phone interview this afternoon with a magazine reporter. I'm excited and a little nervous.*

ROUGHRIDER16: *That's great. Don't be nervous—you'll be amazing.*

SiennaM: *Thanks. I'm always nervous about interviews because some reporters make me sound like the madam of a sex ring or something.*

RoughRider16: *You? That made me lol . . .*

SiennaM: *Google the one by a blogger named Marjorie McDonald. She has a huge following. Her article was supposed to be a tongue in cheek effort at me "harnessing" the unfilled needs of women, but her double entendre skills are lacking and she makes me out as a dominatrix with a bevy of whips, chains, and actual harnesses in my office. I was horrified.*

RoughRider16: *Wow. Yeah, that's shitty, but look at you now. They say even the worst articles create buzz.*

SiennaM: *True . . .*

RoughRider16: *I had a dream about you last night.*

SiennaM: *Do tell . . .*

RoughRider16: *You were in my kitchen, wearing just a T-shirt and panties. I was kissing the back of your neck and sliding my hand under your shirt . . .*

I arch my brows, eager to hear more, but before I can start typing a response to that last message, my office door is thrown open, and a woman with wild, dark curls walks through, glaring at me.

Jane must have stepped out. There's nothing I hate more than walk-ins, but I'll have to handle it.

"Can I help you?" I ask shortly.

"It's all your fault. You ruined everything." Her tone is tearful and shaky, with an undercurrent of rage.

"I'm sorry, do I know you?"

She shakes her head. "I'm Bella Moore. Isaac and I would be together if it wasn't for you and your stupid policies, you bitch."

Shit. Isaac's unbalanced stalker is in my office right now. I reach for my cell phone to call 9–1-1, but Bella lets out an anguished sound.

"Drop. It." She pulls something from her bag, a flash of silver making my blood run cold.

It's a gun, and a pretty big one at that. Suddenly my lax security policies have bitten me in the ass. I hired security for Isaac when this thing with Isabella Moore went down, but I should have locked down the entire office.

I set down the phone, sneaking a hand onto my computer keyboard to type a message to RoughRider.

SIENNAM: *911 my office*

"Put your hands in the air!"

I obey, putting both my hands where she can see them. The crazed look in her eyes terrifies me. I'm not sure she has any awareness of action and consequence right now. She just sees me as the one keeping her from Isaac.

"I'm sorry, Bella." I offer a contrite, gentle apology, though my heart is hammering. "You're absolutely right."

"Why did you do that? Why wouldn't you let him be with me?"

"I guess . . . I just wasn't thinking. I'm sorry."

She puts both hands on the gun, and it looks like she's aiming.

"Please don't," I implore. "Let's talk about this, okay? You seem like a really nice person."

"I am a nice person. But you ruined everything! I might go to jail because of you!"

I glance over at my computer screen, scanning the IMs RoughRider responded with.

ROUGHRIDER16: *What the hell? Are you okay???*

ROUGHRIDER16: *Sienna, answer, please. Are you okay?*

ROUGHRIDER16: *If you don't respond within ten seconds, I'm calling*

911. Please fucking respond.

RoughRider16: *I just called 911 and your office. Say something, Sienna.*

I see movement outside my office through the glass wall. My payroll clerk, Sandy, is staring at me, wide-eyed. She must be the one who got the call from RoughRider and came to check on me.

"What can I do to make this better?" I ask Bella, hoping to defuse this situation without anyone else being endangered.

She shakes her head and glares at me. "I don't know! I can't talk to Isaac anymore. Can you bring him in here so I can talk to him?"

Shit. I can't put Isaac in that situation, but I don't want to upset Bella further.

"I would, but I don't think he's here right now."

"Why not? He always works at this time on Tuesdays."

Her stalking game is strong. I'll just have to bluff my way through this.

"He said he had an appointment out of the office this afternoon. I think he's getting a tattoo."

"Really? Of what? Did he say what?"

"Someone's name, I think?"

Bella breaks into a smile. "My name?"

"Might have been."

"I knew he had feelings for me. I *knew* it."

I try to smile at her, hoping it doesn't come off as terrified as I feel right now. When I look back out the glass wall of my office, Sandy is gone. Suddenly, a uniformed CPD officer shows himself to me, then dodges back out of sight immediately. Bella didn't see him because her back is to the glass wall and door.

"I want to know everything about him." She nods, liking her new idea. "Do you have a file for him? With pictures and information? I want to see it."

"I'll show it to you, but it's not in my office. It's in Human Resources."

She considers, looking at the office door. "Okay, take me there."

Bella puts me in front of her, holding on to a handful of my shirt and shoving the barrel of the gun against my back. We've just made it out the door when she's shoved away from me. I trip forward, landing in the arms of an officer in tactical gear, who sweeps me away as Bella is tackled and disarmed.

The officer takes me to the break room, where I sit down. That's when I start shaking, the terror of the situation finally safe to fully feel. I cry a little and drink some water. Once Bella has been taken away, I go out to the main lobby area of the office to answer questions for the officers there. They've only gotten one question out when Coop comes flying through the elevator doors the moment they open.

"Sienna, thank God." He wraps me in a huge hug, exhaling deeply. "I heard the call come over the radio, and I got here as soon as I could."

I hug him back, his embrace comforting me. "I'm okay, Coop."

Coop's best friend Ryan races up behind him, his whole expression falling with relief when he sees I'm okay.

"You called Ryan?" I give Coop an admonishing look. "That was kind of overkill. I don't need both my big brothers running to my rescue."

Coop furrows his brow and looks at Ryan. "No, I didn't call him. What are you doing here, man? How'd you know?"

Ryan's dark brown eyes are on me, swimming with emotions—apology, relief, fear, and something so intense it takes my breath away.

When it hits me, it hits hard. Ryan knew what was going on without Coop calling him because it was *me* who told him. He was the one who called 9–1-1. The one frantically asking me if I was okay. The one who sent me the flowers. The one who said I mean everything to him.

"No." My lips part with shock and disbelief. "I can't ... Ryan ... it's *you*? You're RoughRider?"

SEVENTEEN

#gutted

RYAN

THE DISAPPOINTMENT IN Sienna's eyes is like a boulder falling on my chest, the weight nearly unbearable. This is what I couldn't bring myself to face—her discovering her secret admirer is me and wishing it were someone else.

"Rough rider?" Coop narrows his gaze on me. "What the hell does that mean?"

"Let's not talk about it here," I say.

"I think we should." His tone is challenging.

My tone is definitive enough to cut him off, though. "I think you should shut up and focus on your sister."

He's sulking as Sienna returns to be questioned by the police. I move to lean my back against a wall in the lobby, alone, so I can process the jumble of thoughts and emotions inside me.

"What the fuck is going on?" Coop hisses in a loud whisper.

Of course, he followed me. Fucker won't rest until he knows the entire story.

"We're not talking about it here."

"Then let's leave."

I glare at him. "I'm not leaving until I know Sienna's okay."

"She's surrounded by cops. I think she'll survive."

"I don't just mean physically okay, douchebag."

Coop leans in, his face inches from mine. "You know who's in danger of not being physically okay? You, when I hear my little sister associating you with the word 'ride.'"

I exhale hard, folding my arms over my chest. "We're not having this conversation here."

"I'll kill you, Ryan. Your guilt is written all over your smug-ass face right now, and I'm gonna strangle the life out of you with my bare hands, you miserable, no-good son of a bitch."

There are two reasons I didn't want Sienna to find out I'm RoughRider—I didn't want to face her disappointment, and I didn't want to face Coop's wrath. He told me a long time ago that she's hands-off. I always respected it—still am, actually, because I haven't laid a hand on his sister. Both of those issues kept me up at night when I considered telling Sienna who I really am, and now here I am, dealing with them at the same time.

"Let's focus on Sienna for now," I say in a level tone.

"Sounds like you've been *overly* focused on her." He scowls at me, his hands clenched into fists.

I take a deep breath, forcing myself to stay silent. Sienna doesn't need any more stress right now, and if Coop and I get into it near cops who don't know how we are around each other, one or both of us may end up in jail.

Coop's next to me, his back also against the wall, and he's muttering without looking at me.

"If you touched my sister, you gutless bastard, I will neuter you while you sleep. I'll crush your fucking nut sac with a hammer. You'll be gutless *and* nutless, you dirty—"

I cut him off. "Shut it, Coop. You sound ridiculous."

"You won't be laughing when I break your fucking nose, asshole."

"Yeah, 'cause I'll just take that, right? I'm stronger and faster than you, and I've been lifting heavy with my team every day, fucker, while you sit around the fire station eating doughnuts."

"Okay, cocksucker, outside. Now."

I turn on him, the first to speak in a tone above an angry, hissed whisper. "Yeah? Because a perceived insult to your sister's honor is one thing, but a comment about the number of doughnuts you eat is worth fighting over?"

Coop's face is red with anger as he pulls up his T-shirt. "Abs." He points at his stomach. "I didn't get those by eating doughnuts all day, asshole."

"Put your shirt down, dumbass." I shake my head, embarrassed by his display.

One of the cops is giving us a side-eye, and I'm not getting kicked out of here without knowing Sienna is okay. The last thirty minutes have probably taken years off my life. I handed my last history class of the day off to an assistant principal and drove to Sienna's office as fast as my truck would go, pounding on the steering wheel with frustration at every red light.

When I couldn't find parking near her office, I took a spot a half mile away and ran the rest of the way. I was beside myself, a caged lion, on the elevator ride up to her office suite. Thoughts raced through my head faster than I could process them. There was one that kept repeating itself:

She has to be okay. I haven't even told her I'm in love with her.

I've loved Sienna in secret for so long that it's become part of me. She's the reason I don't date anymore. I tried for a long time—years, but no other woman affects me the way she does.

Her laugh takes my breath away. Her smile makes my heart race. And seeing her in a skirt . . . well, it really does work me up like nothing else, just as I told her.

Damn, was it good to tell her that. Even though she didn't know it was me, I finally got to be honest with her about my feelings as RoughRider. She's more under my skin than ever now, but it's a high I can't get my fill of.

She was never supposed to know, though. Our messages were a way for me to know her in a way I wanted like nothing else, but never thought I could have. When I read the article about Alpha Mail in the *Sun*, I realized I could contact her without her knowing it was me. The temptation was just too much.

And once I got a look at the side of her I've always wanted to see—the side that's all woman—I couldn't look away.

Coop and I wait in silence until the police finish questioning Sienna, and then he approaches her and offers to take her home.

"No, I'm . . ." She looks around until her eyes lock on mine, and damn if my pulse doesn't pound harder with every passing second. " . . . fine, Coop."

"What's going on between you and Ryan?" he demands, trying his glare on her now.

"It's . . . I don't know." A slight pink flush spreads across her cheeks.

Coop looks back and forth between us, then crosses his arms. "I'm not leaving here till one of you tells me what's going on."

The elevator doors open, and a blond man practically runs to Sienna, looking her over from head to toe.

"I just heard. What the hell did she do now?"

Sienna holds out a hand in an effort to calm him. "I'm fine, Isaac. No one was hurt."

"She pulled a gun on you?" He runs a hand through his hair,

eyes wide with shock.

"Yes, but I'm okay."

"Shit. If I'd been here, she wouldn't have come after you."

"You don't know that. This isn't your fault. She's mentally unstable." Sienna consoles him, ever the level-headed woman I've grown to adore.

Isaac takes a deep breath in and out. "If they don't keep her in jail this time . . ." He shakes his head and looks away.

"Don't get ahead of yourself," Sienna says. "The police officers who interviewed me said they need to talk to you too. So can you go to the station and do that? Then take the rest of the week off, okay? You'll still get paid, and we'll cover your work. Just try to get your mind off all this."

He nods, his expression still somber. I take it this is the guy the woman who got arrested was really after.

As soon as he's out of earshot, Coop looks between Sienna and me again. "Who's gonna tell me? Or should I just assume the worst and kick Ryan's ass as soon as we get outside?"

"Coop." Sienna gives him an admonishing look.

"You're not kicking anybody's ass." I gesture toward the elevator. "I need to talk to Sienna alone, so hit the road."

Coop's eyes bulge with surprise. "Hit the road? The only thing I'm gonna hit is—"

"Enough, Coop," Sienna says firmly. "I'm twenty-eight years old, I can take care of myself. I appreciate you coming here to check on me, but I'm fine."

Coop scowls at me, a vein in his neck standing out. "I'll be waiting for you when you get home."

"You'll be waiting a while, because I have practice till eight. The offensive coaching staff doesn't take it as easy as the defensive."

He doesn't take the bait. "Just call me when you're done."

"I'll get right on that," I say in a wry tone.

"We're not done."

"We are for now."

We have a stare-off for a few seconds, and then he hugs Sienna and leaves. When it's just the two of us, neither of us seems to know what to say.

"Do you, uh . . . want to talk in my office?" she offers, an awkward expression on her face.

"If you're up for it. Are you still feeling shaken up?"

She shakes her head and tucks a section of dark red hair behind her ear. "No, I'm okay. We can . . . let's go talk."

I follow her down the hallway, not focusing much on my surroundings even though it's the first time I've been to her office. My gaze is narrowed on the way her legs look in her skirt and the way it hugs her ass just the right way. Lucky fucking skirt.

"This is me," she says, standing aside as she opens the glass door of a large, bright office.

"After you."

She steps inside and I follow, the door closing behind us on its own.

Her office is painted a pale turquoise shade, the walls adorned with black and white photos of ornate old buildings. A bookshelf behind her large wood desk is filled with paperbacks, knickknacks and framed photos.

She leans back on the front of her desk and locks eyes with me. "Why did you do it?"

"Why?"

Doesn't she know why? Her expression is confused and crestfallen. I knew she'd be disappointed, but she looks completely devastated right now.

"Was it a joke?" she asks softly.

Blood rushes to my head as I process her words. I'm so taken aback I can't even speak for a few seconds. "A joke? You think the whole thing was a joke to me?"

"I don't know, Ryan. That's what I'm asking."

Her hurt expression guts me. Never did I expect this. I have to set her straight.

"No, it wasn't a joke, Sienna. I've been in love with you for a long time. Years. I knew I could never tell you, but I saw a chance to get to know you in a way I never thought I'd be able to, and I . . . I took it. I never meant for you to find out."

"That's not possible." She shakes her head slightly, her brow furrowed.

"What's not possible?"

"That you're in love with me. You don't even think of me that way. I've always been like a little sister to you, same as Coop."

My breath catches in my throat as I try to figure out how to tell her the truth. "It was that way when we were kids. But things changed for me, Pup. I remember the exact moment it happened, and—"

"When?"

I sigh heavily. "When Coop and I were seniors in college, and he asked me to come over and help him move an entertainment center for your parents on a weekend. You came down the stairs dressed for prom, and . . ." I can still see her that day, radiant in a dark green sleeveless dress, and the memory renders me speechless for a second. " . . . that was it. I was so goddamn jealous of your date when he touched you, and it wasn't a brotherly kind of thing anymore. It was because I wanted you for myself."

"Ryan," she says in a breathless tone. "That was ten years ago."

I nod and fold my arms over my chest. "Yeah."

"But you . . ." She shakes her head. "You've been with women since then. There was that time I saw you downtown with that blonde a few years ago."

"I knew it would never happen between us, Sienna. I knew you didn't see me that way, and I knew Coop wouldn't let me even try if you did. So I tried to shake the feeling by dating other women, but it never worked. I started to feel bad about it, like I was using them, so a few years ago, I stopped."

"Stopped dating? Altogether?"

"Yeah."

"But you're so . . . I mean, you're in your prime."

I shrug. "So are you."

We just look at each other for a few seconds in silence. The look on her face is killing me. There's shock and disbelief, but not a hint of happiness or hope. It's just as I expected, but it still hurts like a bitch.

"I'm sorry, Sienna," I manage. "I'd never intentionally mislead or disappoint you."

She nods, looking dazed. "I wish I could . . . I don't even know what to say."

"I get it. You don't think of me that way."

She looks down at the ground, seemingly ashamed. "No, I don't. I'm so sorry."

I knew the truth, but I never wanted to hear her say it. At least I had an ounce of hope before, and our limited interactions when we saw each other through Coop. Now, things will always be awkward between us, and my friendship with Coop is probably shot too.

Fuck. Why did I ever send that first email?

"I'm gonna go," I say, needing air, space . . . anything but that crushed expression on her face.

I turn and leave the office, knowing it's no one's fault but my own that things will never be the same.

EIGHTEEN

#mrlennox

RYAN

A COUPLE DAYS later, I'm standing in front of my American History class, leaning back against the front of my desk, when I completely forget where I was going in my lecture.

"So, uh . . . Hoover . . ."

"You okay, Mr. Lennox?" a girl in the front row of desks asks.

"Yeah, I'm fine. I just . . . lost my train of thought."

"That's 'cause this Hoover guy is boring," a mouthy guy in the back of the room cracks.

"Herbert Hoover was anything but boring. He was a self-made millionaire who arguably fed more people and saved more lives than any single man in history. He even had a sport named after him. You ever have a sport named after you, Declan?"

He scoffs as students around him snicker.

"Hell, I'm only fifteen. Gimme time." His grin is arrogant. "I'll probably have a whole state named after me or some shit."

I fold my arms across my chest, waiting patiently as Declan's friends laugh and fist bump him for his outburst.

When the noise has died down, I say, "As you will recall from the talk I gave on the first day of class, and the syllabus you signed, Declan, you just scored yourself a special assignment. I'll be looking for a one-thousand-word paper on the origin and historical uses of the profane word you just used on my desk Monday morning."

Now the snickers are directed *at* Declan, which he's not such a fan of.

"What the . . . ?" He gives me an openmouthed stare.

"Careful, or you'll have two papers to write."

He clamps his mouth shut. In the eight years I've been teaching, I've often had to assign the profanity paper to one student, early in the school year. I've never had to assign a second one, though.

The bell rings, and my class clears out. Declan keeps his head down, not even trying to give me a dirty look. Between my job as my high school's football coach and the tattoos visible on one of my arms when I'm wearing a short-sleeved shirt, most smartass boys don't run their mouths to me. And if they do, they usually regret it.

I don't have a bad temper. It's the opposite, actually. I'm unfazed by dumb adolescent behavior, but I do call it out and enforce repercussions. Teaching and coaching are very similar—it's all about action and consequences. My boys know if I tell them we're conditioning, it's gonna be a long, hard session, but I'll be right in there beside them.

Coaching football is the only reason I still have abs. The rest of my body is in peak physical shape too. If Sienna wanted to be with a guy based on looks, I'd have a damn good shot. But she's a smart, amazing woman who wants it all. And she can't have it all with a man she thinks of as a brother.

I wouldn't give up my past with Sienna for anything, even though it means I can't have the future I want with her. Any other man she's with will never know her the way I do.

I was there when she pulled out a loose tooth during a neighborhood baseball game, stuck it in her pocket right there in the batter's circle, and continued with her at-bat. She hit a single, too.

When her grandma passed away, I sat next to her at the funeral, sweaty and awkward in a suit my mom made me wear, and she leaned her head on my shoulder for a few seconds as she cried. At the time, I was silently put off by my best buddy's younger sister leaning against me with a runny nose and tear-stained cheeks, but now . . . I'd give anything to be her comfort.

The next time I saw her crying, I wasn't disgusted—I was pissed. Coop and I were sixteen then, and we were playing football in his front yard when Sienna came running down the sidewalk and up the driveway, sobbing. She was crying so hard she was hiccupping, but Coop finally got out of her that a boy from her class had asked her to be his girlfriend, taken her behind the school to mess around with her—which included putting his dirty little hands up her shirt—and then promptly dumped her when she told him to stop. Coop and I paid a visit to that twelve-year-old piece of shit and helped him see the error of his ways.

Protecting her has been second nature to me for a long time, but a decade ago, it stopped being brotherly for me. I'd walk through fire for Sienna because I'm deeply, irrationally in love with her.

My days of fantasizing about her over dinner at her parents' house are long gone, though. Things will be awkward as fuck from here on out, all because of my stupid idea to get closer to her as RoughRider.

I'm still ignoring Coop. He's been messaging me constantly, though he seems to have cooled off a bit. There's no way I'm dealing with his bullshit anytime soon. Sienna rejected me, which hurt like hell even though it's what I expected. I'm not apologizing to

Coop for loving Sienna. It's outside my control, and I'd die before I hurt her.

My last hour of the day is my planning period, so I sit down at my desk and force myself to focus on grading papers. I'm almost halfway through the stack when my Foxy app dings with a new message.

My heart stalls for a couple seconds. The only person I use that app to message with is Sienna. I grab the phone and read the lines on the screen.

SIENNAM: *Ryan, are you there?*

ROUGHRIDER16: *Yeah, I'm here. Hi.*

SIENNAM: *Hi. Is this a good time?*

ROUGHRIDER16: *Yeah. How are you?*

SIENNAM: *I'm good. You?*

ROUGHRIDER16: *I'm okay.*

SIENNAM: *Was that enough small talk?*

ROUGHRIDER16: *More than enough for me. How are you, really?*

SIENNAM: *That makes me think of you asking me, "Who are you, really?" But you already knew, didn't you? You've known me almost my entire life.*

ROUGHRIDER16: *No, I didn't know you the way I wanted to.*

SIENNAM: *Do you know me better now?*

ROUGHRIDER16: *Better than I did, but not as well as I'd like.*

SIENNAM: *It's taken me a few days to let things sink in. I was so shocked, Ryan. In some ways, I still am.*

ROUGHRIDER16: *You were never supposed to know. When you said*

911, though, all I could think about was getting to you to make sure you were okay.

SIENNAM: *That seems a little cruel to me. Professing these feelings for me as RoughRider, making me have feelings back, and you never planned to reveal yourself?*

ROUGHRIDER16: *You had feelings back?*

SIENNAM: *Couldn't you tell?*

ROUGHRIDER16: *No . . . sorry.*

SIENNAM: *It feels like you were leading me on.*

ROUGHRIDER16: *That was never my intent.*

SIENNAM: *What was your intent?*

ROUGHRIDER16: *To see a side of you I didn't think I'd ever get to see.*

SIENNAM: *You're Coop's best friend, and my friend too. I care for you and would never want to hurt you. I hope you know that.*

ROUGHRIDER16: *You don't need to do this. I got the message—you're not interested in me.*

SIENNAM: *I just can't see Ryan Lennox and RoughRider as one and the same. I can't even wrap my mind around you being interested in me. I'm just Coop's lost puppy dog little sister. You can get any woman you want.*

ROUGHRIDER16: *I want you.*

SIENNAM: *I'm moody and impatient.*

ROUGHRIDER16: *You're determined. That's a good thing.*

SIENNAM: *I'm independent and terrible at relationships.*

ROUGHRIDER16: *I know who you are, Sienna. I love your*

independence. And you're terrible at relationships because you choose losers who don't treat you right.

SIENNAM: *How would you know?*

ROUGHRIDER16: *Coop. For years, I've gritted my teeth as he told me about the latest douchebag to hurt you.*

RoughRider 16: Still there?

SIENNAM: *I'm here. I just don't know what to say.*

ROUGHRIDER16: *You don't have to say anything. You don't owe me anything. I just hope you know how sorry I am. I'd never hurt you. What I did was selfish.*

SIENNAM: *You don't need to be sorry. I'm sorry, though. It's not you.*

ROUGHRIDER16: *You're killin' me, Pup . . .*

SIENNAM: *I'm sorry.*

ROUGHRIDER16: *Stop saying that. :/*

SIENNAM: *Okay, new subject . . . you're a history teacher, aren't you?*

ROUGHRIDER16: *Yep.*

SIENNAM: *So what was the Bob and John promotion thing about? You don't have any employees, do you?*

ROUGHRIDER16: *It was about two players on my football team. I took your advice, btw, and "John" is killing it as a starter.*

SIENNAM: *Not his real name?*

ROUGHRIDER16: *No. His name is Brendan.*

ROUGHRIDER16: *Hey, that psycho who pulled a gun on you—is she in jail?*

SIENNAM: *Yes. She hasn't been able to make bail.*

ROUGHRIDER16: *Good. What will do you if she does get out?*

SIENNAM: *I don't know. I should have a security system installed at my house, I suppose.*

ROUGHRIDER16: *You should. What kind of locks do you have on your doors?*

SIENNAM: *There's a lock on the door handle and a chain on both doors. We always lock them.*

ROUGHRIDER16: *You need deadbolts.*

SIENNAM: *Good idea. I'll ask the security company to install them.*

ROUGHRIDER16: *I'll do it. I can come by tonight after practice.*

ROUGHRIDER16: *It's not a backward effort to see you. I'm genuinely concerned.*

SIENNAM: *If you're able to do it, I'd appreciate it. I know you're concerned. Thanks.*

ROUGHRIDER16: *If you want shooting lessons, I can teach you. I have a handgun you can borrow.*

SIENNAM: *OMG no. I don't want a gun in my house. I'd never be comfortable shooting one.*

ROUGHRIDER16: *You'd get comfortable if that maniac client broke in to your house . . .*

SIENNAM: *I'll think about it.*

ROUGHRIDER16: *No, you won't. I know you, remember?*

SIENNAM: *You're right, I won't . . .*

ROUGHRIDER16: *Be careful, okay? You've seen what this lady's capable of.*

SIENNAM: *I will. Promise.*

ROUGHRIDER16: *I'll install a camera at your front door too, so you can see who's there before opening it.*

SIENNAM: *You know how to do that?*

ROUGHRIDER16: *It's not hard.*

SIENNAM: *Let me know what I owe you for the supplies.*

ROUGHRIDER16: *Nothing. I just want you to be safe.*

SIENNAM: *Promise me we won't let it be awkward between us now.*

ROUGHRIDER16: *Promise.*

SIENNAM: *Okay. See you tonight?*

ROUGHRIDER16: *See you then.*

NINETEEN

#likelukeandleia

WHEN I OPEN my front door and see Ryan standing there in black shorts, a gray "Oakhurst Football" T-shirt spanning his broad chest, his dark hair damp from a shower, it's definitely awkward.

In a way, it's like I'm seeing him for the first time. The tattoos he's had on one arm since right after he finished college seem different somehow. The dark stubble on his face doesn't make me react the same way as it would on my brother's face this time. My insides are a melted mess, and the intense look he's giving me only makes it worse.

"Can I come in, Pup?"

I force my mouth to close and give him a smile. "Yeah . . . sorry."

He walks in and sets his toolbox next to my door, looking at the doorframe in silent, Ryan-like fashion. He's always been the sort who doesn't talk just to fill space. If Ryan speaks, it's because he has something important to say.

But RoughRider liked to chat, even about small, insignificant stuff. It strikes me yet again how different the two personas seem. Maybe I don't really know either of them. Or maybe I have to know both to know the whole man.

Do I want to know the whole man, though? Really know him, inside and out? What turns him on and sets him off? Before meeting RoughRider, I would have said no. But now . . . I'm not sure.

I sit down on the couch and grab a magazine, not really reading it but wanting to look busy. This is *beyond* awkward for me. I'm picturing Ryan sitting in his bed as I sat in mine, messaging me about the dirty things he wants to do to me.

I'd kiss you until your lips were tingling and your chest was rising and falling as you panted my name.

I know of some great ways to work out stress before bed.

You'd clench around me really tight and I'd feel you start to spasm.

My cheeks burn with embarrassment at the memories. At least, I *think* it's embarrassment.

It's at least forty percent embarrassment. And I'm not ready to admit the other sixty percent of the reason I'm warm right now.

This is Ryan Lennox. Coop's best friend. I was arriving home with my mom when she busted the two of them sneaking girls out of our basement when they were sophomores in high school. They both had messed-up hair and nervous smiles, the smells of Axe body spray and guilt rolling off of them.

Ryan witnessed my humiliation when I tried to leave the house in sixth grade wearing a white T-shirt and a black bra. He and Coop had snickered when my mom insisted I change into the training bra she'd gotten me.

I hated that term then, and I hate it still. What sort of training do breasts need, anyway? I'm pretty sure my disdain for the term stems from that day my mom threw it around in front of my older brother and his friend with no regard for my pubescent embarrassment.

"Why are you reading my *Junior Woodsman* magazine?" Jack

demands, entering the living room with a skeptical look my way.

"I . . . uh . . ." I glance down at the magazine I absently grabbed and sigh through my nose. "I like foxes. I thought this article sounded good."

I chance a glance at Ryan and swear I see a hint of a smile tugging on the corners of his lips.

"Who's he?" Jack frowns in Ryan's direction.

I stand up and put the magazine back on the table. "Have you guys never met?"

Ryan looks up from his toolbox. "We met at your parents' house one year at Christmas, but Jack was just a little guy then." He stands up and extends a hand to Jack. "You probably don't remember me. I'm Ryan."

"Hi," Jack says solemnly, putting his hand in Ryan's.

Ryan smiles down at him. "Not bad, but try again and grip my hand tighter this time. Like this."

They shake hands again, and then Jack furrows his brow and squeezes Ryan's hand in a tighter grip.

"Nice." Ryan gives him an approving smile. "That's a man's handshake right there."

Jack's expression lights up. "What are you doing to the door?"

"I'm gonna put in some deadbolt locks. I have to drill into the frame and the door."

Jack nods his approval. "I know how to use a hammer if you need help."

"Yeah? I could use some help, actually."

Ryan explains every tool to Jack and shows him how to use each one. He corrects him gently and praises him liberally. Jack has trouble grasping the small pieces Ryan passes him, and he drops them often. He can't help it—the loss of motor skills is part of the disease that's going to take him from us one day. But Ryan takes it in stride, telling Jack it's okay every time he gets frustrated because he let something else fall to the floor.

Carmen is leaning against the doorframe to the kitchen, watching them, tears shining in her eyes. I hope they're happy tears over Jack's excitement, but I know how hard it is for her to watch his disease slowly steal away his ability to do things.

Jack doesn't remember his dad, and he doesn't have many male role models. Carmen has told me before that he asks her why his dad isn't around, and it breaks her heart every time. No matter how many times she tells him it's not his fault, he doesn't seem to buy it.

"If he loves me, why doesn't he want to see me?"

When Carmen told me Jack said that to her one night as she was tucking him in for bed, she cried and then I did too. She's an amazing mother to Jack, but she can't be a father to him too, no matter how much she tries.

She considered telling him his dad passed away, so at least Jack wouldn't know his dad is alive and well but doesn't care about seeing him, but she couldn't bring herself to lie to him.

It takes Ryan at least twice as long to install the front door deadbolt with Jack's help than it would have taken alone. Carmen starts dinner as they move on to the back door, and I pace around the living room by myself.

RoughRider is in my house right now. Specifically, he's in my kitchen, teaching Jack how to use a drill. I don't know if that's crazier than the fact that he's actually Ryan. It all seems kind of crazy right now.

Ryan is a good man. He's patient but firm, and he was made to be a teacher and a coach. I've always known that side of him. He played football in high school and college, and he never messed around with any behaviors that could get him kicked out of the sport he loves. He's like a brother to Coop—always there, for fun times and tough ones.

I never thought I'd know this other side of Ryan. His RoughRider side is brooding yet sweet, impatient at times yet . . . willing to go without women if he can't have the one he wants. And I still can't believe that's *me*.

I didn't think about who I *really* am until Ryan asked me as RoughRider. I'm realizing I also never thought about what I really want in a man before him. I spent so much time focusing on what I *didn't* want and founding Alpha Mail based on those things, that what I *do* want didn't seem important.

Realizing what I don't want in a man and opening a business because of it changed my life. But pacing in my living room, I consider for the first time that getting in touch with what I do want in a man could change my life even more.

I stop walking and take a deep breath, then walk into the kitchen, talking before Ryan even has a chance to realize I'm there.

"Why didn't you tell me sooner? Why did you keep this to yourself for . . . a decade?"

He looks up from his crouched position next to the doorframe. "You want to talk about this now?"

His tone is surprised, but level. That's Ryan. Always calm, cool, and collected, even when I'm feeling a little unhinged.

"Why not?" I throw my hands in the air.

The hint of a smile comes back as he takes a part to the deadbolt that Jack was holding for him.

"I didn't tell you because I knew you didn't feel that way for me." Ryan looks at the piece he's drilling rather than at me, the patience in his tone grating on my nerves.

"How did you know that? Why did you think you were better at knowing how I feel than *I* am?"

"I was right, wasn't I?"

"Well . . ." I fold my arms and consider. "Now that we're twenty-eight and thirty-two, yeah, but . . . maybe if you had said something back then . . ."

"I didn't know for sure what I was feeling. I wasn't sure if it was just attraction or . . . love."

Jack inhales sharply. "Love? You love her?"

Ryan nods. "I do."

"You guys are like Princess Leia and Han Solo." Jack looks back and forth between us and grins.

"For her, it's more like Leia and Luke Skywalker," Ryan says.

Jack gives me a dirty look. "What?"

I throw my hands up in frustration. "I don't even know what that means!"

"He's not your brother." Jack shakes his head and then turns to Ryan. "Are you?"

"No," Ryan says it emphatically. "I'm definitely not."

Carmen intervenes. "Jack, let's run to the store and pick up some ice cream."

"But I'm helping!"

"Well . . ." She looks from Ryan to me. "Maybe Ryan wouldn't mind taking a break until we get back?"

Ryan stands. "Sure, I can do that."

Jack looks up at him. "You promise not to work on it until I get back?"

"Promise."

Carmen grabs her purse and keys, hustling Jack out of the house. And now that we have privacy, Ryan and I just stare at each other across the room in silence.

"Tell me what's really on your mind, Sienna," Ryan says.

I furrow my brow and run a hand through my hair.

"Everything's different now. You've never called me Sienna."

"You want me to keep calling you Pup?" He gives me an amused grin.

"I don't know." I sigh heavily and sit down on a kitchen chair.

"Hey," he says softly. "It's gonna take some time for things to be like they used to be between us. But we'll get there."

His eyes are a dark caramel shade. Why have I never noticed that before? They're warm and intense at the same time.

"I wish . . ." I bury my face in my hands. "I'm just not there in my life right now. I'm so focused on my business, and I don't even know what I want in a man. I just realized a few minutes ago that I've never really thought about what I want, because I've been so busy not wanting anyone."

"And that's okay. You don't have to have all the answers right now. You're young, and your business is booming. Just take it easy on that part of your life."

"Who are you?" My voice is louder than intended. "One minute, you're in love with me, and the next, you're offering me indifferent, brotherly advice."

"I am in love with you, but I know it's one-sided. Look . . ." He rests his hands on his hips and looks from the floor to the ceiling before leveling his gaze at me. "It's my fault you're confused about all this. I'm not waiting or anything, so don't think that. I don't want you to offer me a mercy date. I'd turn you down if you did. My feelings for you would always be stronger than yours for me. I think it's better for me never to have you at all than to have you in a halfhearted way."

I open my mouth to speak, close it, then try again. "So you're saying you love me, but you don't want me?"

"Pretty much. I won't be with a woman who isn't all in, and you'd never be all in with me. I think seeing your disappointment that day in your office when you realized it was me, and hearing you say you don't share my feelings was actually . . . good for me. I can move on now."

"You can move on." Dazed, I shake my head and stand up.

"We both can. I know this whole thing threw you for a loop, and I've apologized for it. I don't know what else to do."

I'm hurt. Irrationally, deeply, foolishly hurt. I don't want him to see the tears in my eyes, so I just turn and leave the room, not stopping until I'm upstairs curled up on my bed.

I cry. Because I'm confused, because I hurt Ryan, because he unknowingly hurt me back. I even cry for the loss of RoughRider, even though he's not really gone. What I really want right now is to message him and have an IM date. It's ironic that he's right downstairs and I've never felt so far away from him.

An IM date isn't happening, though. It'll never happen again. What the hell . . . I cry over that too.

WHEN CARMEN WALKS into the room later, I only recognize her outline by the glow of the hallway light.

"Hey." I sit up, my mouth dry and my eyes sore from crying.

"Hey." She sits down on the end of my bed.

"I must have fallen asleep. What time is it?" I sit up and switch on the lamp beside my bed.

"Nine-thirty."

"Oh, wow. Is Ryan still here?"

"He left around nine. And he let Jack keep his tape measure." She smiles.

I close my eyes, our earlier conversation coming back in a flood.

"Want to talk about it?" Carmen asks.

"I just don't know how to be with him anymore. I don't know how to even think about him. It was one thing when I didn't have to see him or talk to him, but—"

She cuts me off. "Do you really not see how amazing he is?"

"No . . . I mean, yes. I know he's great."

"He's more than great. And he's in love with you. So give him a chance, Sienna."

I sigh heavily. "That's just not how I see him."

"Open your eyes, then. Stop being so stubborn."

"You don't even know Ryan. You saw him with Jack tonight, and now you think I should date him?"

She narrows her eyes slightly. "When you told me he was your secret admirer, I didn't even remember seeing him at your parents' house several years ago. I trusted you to judge whether he's right for you or not."

"And what? You don't now?" I give her an incredulous look.

"No. Not after seeing the two of you together."

"So since we make a cute couple, I should be with him?"

"No, dumbass. Because I've never seen you like that over any man."

"Like what? Confused?"

"Emotionally invested."

I roll my eyes. "Carmen. Of course, I'm emotionally invested. I've known Ryan most of my life. This whole situation is . . . sticky. Not just because of me and him, but also my brother."

"Yeah, not buying it."

"Not buying what?"

She holds up a hand. "Not so loud, you'll wake up Jack."

"Sorry."

"So tell me what happened after Jack and I escaped the kitchen full of pent-up feelings."

I glare at her. "Nothing much. I told him I'm confused and I don't know what I want, and he . . . pretty much told me not to want him."

"What?" Carmen gives me a skeptical look.

"He said he'd turn me down if I wanted to go out with him."
I rub a loose thread from my comforter between my thumb and
forefinger, looking at it to avoid Carmen's perceptive gaze. "Because he knows I'd never be all in, and he wouldn't want me if it
was halfhearted."

"Well, I can understand that, actually."

"He's over it." I shrug. "So that's that."

"Are *you* over it?"

"Pretty much."

Carmen scoffs. "You lying sack of shit. Why do you even bother
trying to lie to me? I know you too well for that."

"I'm not lying. Getting completely over it will take time." I
look up at her.

"Right. That's why your eyes are swollen and red. Because
you're *so* getting over it."

I feel a flare of aggravation. "Like I said, it takes time."

"No, Sienna. With time, your feelings will get easier to ignore.
You'll bury yourself in work and Jack, and eventually, you'll be
in your thirties. Then you'll keep ignoring your feelings and tell
yourself you're just a modern, independent woman until one day,
he marries someone else. And then you'll come crying to me about
how stupid you were, but it'll be too late."

I just look at her, taken aback not just by what she said, but
the anger I hear in her tone.

"I love you, but sometimes you just don't get it." She continues.
"Some people live their whole lives without someone looking at
them like he looks at you. The way you came storming into the
kitchen, and the way he took it all in stride, not blinking an eye
when he said he loves you in front of two people he doesn't even

know . . . He's sweet and honest and strong—and *ridiculously* hot."

I'm about to respond when Carmen silences me with her pointed finger. "Do *not* make some stupid crack about how I should date him if I think he's so great. I'm serious."

It's kind of scary how well she knows me. My shoulders sink as I say, "I know."

"I don't care what he said after we left, he is in love with you. Crazy, stupid love. You better think long and hard about whether you want to let go of that so easily."

"I do feel something," I admit, my voice barely above a whisper as I stare at the loose thread on the comforter again. "But I don't know if it's enough. I don't know if I have it in me to feel that crazy, stupid love for any man. I've been dumped on and disappointed so many times."

"I know." Carmen's tone is sympathetic now. "But not by him."

"He wants me to love him back with everything he feels for me, and . . . that would take time for me. Ryan wants all or nothing."

She sighs softly. "That's a lot to ask, you're right. But think about it. That's all I'm saying."

When she approaches to hug me, I close my eyes and take comfort in her embrace. Carmen is my rock in so many ways, and I'm hers. I've never even considered letting a man audition for that role.

Maybe I need to.

TWENTY

#anewhope

RYAN

I RARELY DRINK, which is probably why the beer I just finished has me feeling extra mellow. When I set my empty bottle down on the bar, the bartender approaches with a smile.

"Another one, sweetie?"

I put up a hand and shake my head. "No, I'm good, thanks."

"That one's on the house." She winks and turns to walk to the other end of the bar, adding an extra sway to her step.

If a random hookup would help, I'd take her home with me tonight. But I discovered a long time ago that sex with other women leaves me feeling hollow. I compare them to Sienna and end up feeling guilty as fuck for using them just to get her off my mind.

I've got bigger things to think about anyway. Coop's due here any minute so I can tell him about the RoughRider debacle. I owe him that. Owed it to him sooner than this, actually, but I haven't been able to bring myself to tell him until now.

He walks into the bar right on time, not smiling as I'm used to, but sliding onto the stool and arching his brows.

"Beer? You never drink."

I shrug. "Sometimes I have a beer. I needed to mellow out before you got here."

He rests his elbows on the bar and looks down at the scratched wood surface. "I've waited weeks for you to finally get the balls to tell me what's up with you and Sienna, so don't drag it out. Fucking spit it out, man."

I wish I had asked for another beer as I exhale heavily and nod. There's no getting around it—I have to come clean.

So I do. I start with that day ten years ago when Sienna walked downstairs in that green prom dress, and I saw her—truly saw her—for the first time. I tell him about the jealousy that burns inside me every time he talks about her dating someone. And finally, I share the details of becoming RoughRider, but I leave out the specifics of our conversations. Those aren't between anyone but Sienna and me.

Coop only looks at me a few times as I spill my guts, his jaw set in a tense line. When the bartender comes by for his order, he asks for a beer *and* a shot. I know him well enough to be sure that means he's pissed.

"But none of it really matters anyway, because she doesn't feel the same way." My shoulders sink as I finally reach the end of my confession.

"You're sure?"

I narrow my eyes at him, feeling a rare rise of anger. "Yeah, I'm sure. She told me."

He shakes his head as he takes it all in for a few seconds.

"This whole time? Ten years?"

"Yeah."

"But . . ." He furrows his brow. "What about that one chick? Alisa? You were really into her."

I shrug. "Into her, yeah. But not in love with her. I knew Sienna didn't see me the same way I see her and I didn't want to give up sex forever, so I dated other women."

Coop's shot arrives, and he downs it. "But you haven't dated anyone for a while now. You're like a priest or something."

"It didn't feel right, using other women because I couldn't have her."

He gives me an incredulous look. "I'm just . . . I don't know, man. My instinct was to say you only want her because you know you can't have her, but . . . I don't know."

My single note of laughter is unamused. "It's fucking miserable, Coop. For real. I wish I didn't feel this way about your little sister, but I do. I just wait for the day she marries some other guy, and I can finally . . . maybe . . . let go."

"You guys aren't talking anymore, then?"

"I went over there a few nights ago to install deadbolts on her doors. I can't sleep at night because I'm so worried about that psycho bitch coming to her house."

"She's still in jail. I've got a buddy at CPD who will call me the minute she makes bail . . . if she ever does."

I nod, slightly relieved. "That's good."

"Was it awkward between you guys when you were over there?"

"Yeah. She was . . . I don't know, I guess, emotional?"

Coop laughs, his eyes bright. "Noooo. Sienna? Never."

"I know it, but damned if I don't like her fire. I really do."

"What'd you guys say to each other?"

"I told her I'm moving on and that I don't want a mercy date with her."

Coop furrows his brow again. "She offered that?"

"No, but she's . . . confused. I felt like I needed to end the suffering for both of us, so I told her I'd only want her if she was all in. I don't think Sienna's capable of being all in with any man."

"Not right now, no. She's been shit on, man. Had guys tell her they wanted a relationship and then ditch out after she slept with them."

A hot tingle of jealousy creeps down my spine. "I don't want to hear about any guys she slept with."

"It's been a while. She pretty much gave up and threw herself into Alpha Mail. It's kinda ironic that her successful business is based on failed relationships. That's a big part of who she is and what she believes."

"She chooses assholes." I scrub a hand down my face, feeling caged up on this barstool.

Coop turns to me. "She knows that. Why do you think she stopped dating altogether? It's not just that she doesn't trust men—she doesn't trust herself either."

"That's a damn shame. She's one of the smartest people I know."

"You want my advice?"

I laugh and rest my elbows on the bar. "I figured your advice would be to take a long walk off a short pier."

"I'm not as much of an asshole as you think." Coop gives me a pointed look. "If you ever used or hurt my sister, I'd kick your ass, and our friendship would be over. Don't fucking tell me I couldn't do it or talk shit about your muscles and your fitness. If I was pissed enough, I'd definitely be able to beat your ass."

"I'll concede that. But trust me, I'm hurting more on the inside right now than you could ever make me hurt on the outside."

He wrinkles his face with disgust. "Christ. This thing you have for my sister turned you into a pussy."

I shoot him a glare. "Fuck you. It hurts like a bitch, okay? It's not a passing thing. I've been in love with her for a decade."

"I get it. Now back to my advice . . . Is this the one woman you want more than anyone else in the world?"

"Yes."

"You'd walk through fire for her?"

"I would."

"Then why is it asking too much to be patient with her? You told her all or nothing? If you love her, you'll wait. Loving her means taking her as she is, commitment-phobic, overly emotional, and overwhelmed that you kept this from her for ten years."

I stare down at my empty beer bottle, processing his words. "I said it to let her off the hook."

"Why do you assume she wants off the hook?"

"Because that day in her office, she said she doesn't feel that way about me."

Coop scoffs. "You were expecting her to say she loves you back, ten seconds after she found out you went behind her back like that?"

"I don't know." I rub my forehead, the beer swirling around in my stomach now. "I've never considered that she could ever feel the same way I do. I'm not like the assfucks she dates. They're all pretentious suits with small dicks and big mouths."

"Yeah, and none of 'em are with her, are they?"

I turn my face to look at him. "You think I have a shot with her?"

"I don't know. But I know you, and I know her, and if you really love her, you won't puss out and lie to her. Be a man."

He stands up and reaches for his wallet. "I have to go. I'm helping a guy from work pour some concrete."

"I've got it." I take out my own wallet and set a few bills on the bar.

I stand up to walk out with him, his words still ringing in my ears. This isn't what I was expecting. I thought Coop would rip me a new one and tell me to stay the fuck away from Sienna.

It's in my nature to think things through, and I need time to consider what he said. Am I being unfair to Sienna? Just the thought gives me heartburn.

What would I do if she had a shred of romantic interest in me? Not that she does, but if she did . . . What if she had a gallon of love for me, when I have an ocean for her?

I'd work my ass off to grow that shred. I'd do everything I said to her in those emails—show her with my actions that I love her with everything I am. A shred isn't much compared to my feelings for her, but it's something.

If I at least had that, it could be a start.

TWENTY-ONE

#sugarmama

SIENNA

EVERYONE'S ATTENTION IS focused on the blinking cursor on the large projector screen in front of the room.

"What's a good response here?" I ask the team of three-dozen men. "Just throw something out there. There are no wrong answers."

"Just . . . thinking about you?" a guy in the front row volunteers.

"Good thought, but you don't want to lay it on so thick." I look back up at the question on the screen he's trying to answer, "Hey, what are you doing?"

Gretchen and I are in New York running an exercise to train the New York team. It's been a whirlwind week since the launch of this branch was announced. Client sign-ups exceeded all expectations, and my hiring team is working overtime to bring quality alphas on board.

Every man in this first batch of alphas already has a full client roster. The response is exciting, but also overwhelming. The investors have stressed how much they want Alpha Mail to be out front early, before imitation businesses can swallow up our prospective market.

"So you don't want to lie," I say, looking out at them. "Or I guess you don't want to give an answer that's not possible. If you're sitting in your office here, you don't want to tell the client you're at the gym working out. It's all about a fantasy, but you don't want to deceive."

I reach for the keyboard to type out an answer to Gretchen's latest question. She's handling the client end of the conversation from her laptop on the other side of the room, and I'm working on the alpha side from my end.

"Just got in a workout and got some coffee," I say aloud as I type. "How are you this morning, beautiful?"

I look out over the group of new employees, paying attention to who seems to be listening and who looks disinterested. The New York HR team is supposed to be doing the same from their row of chairs along one side of the room, but I want to make sure they're paying close attention.

"So," I continue, "you usually want to shift the focus back on to the client. Our most satisfied clients like conversations that focus on them, whether it's their day-to-day lives, their frustrations, or their sexual desires. If they ask about you, answer, but remember—no overly personal details, as you read in your orientation guide. We have suggestions listed there for how to deflect those questions."

Gretchen waves to get my attention and taps her watch, signaling that it's lunchtime.

"Okay, so we're going to break for lunch, which is being catered in the other conference room," I tell the group. "And after lunch, Kell from the Chicago office will do a client chat live in here for us."

The room empties quickly, and soon it's just Gretchen and me.

"It's going well," she says, sitting down next to me.

"They seem like a good bunch. Kell will be a better teacher than I am."

Gretchen reaches for the paper cup of coffee she brought over with her, glances at it, then sets it down again.

"I'm gonna go catch a nap on that couch in your office," she says with a sheepish smile. "Sleep sounds better than food right now."

"Take as long as you need. We only got like four hours of sleep last night. I promise we'll quit earlier tonight."

She gives me a skeptical look.

"Promise." I laugh and reach for my own cup of lukewarm coffee.

"I don't mind working late. It's exciting to see this place taking off. It's even bigger than the Chicago office."

"I talked to Sheryl in accounting this morning, and you'll have a very nice bonus coming with your next paycheck."

Gretchen's face lights up. "Thank you. I'm not here because I expected that. I like traveling to new places and helping you."

"I know. But you're great at what you do, and I plan to keep you for a very long time. The way to do that is to show you how much I appreciate you, rather than just telling you."

I prefer actions to words. I remember reading that, not knowing it was actually Ryan, and thinking he might actually be something special. And it's stayed with me. I'm working on showing my executive team how much I value them rather than just patting them on the back.

Gretchen gets up, grabs her bag, and heads for my office, dumping her nearly empty coffee cup in the trash on the way out. I know she's exhausted—I am too—but hopefully, that bonus will help when she sees it in her bank account Friday morning.

I should go in and have lunch with the New York team. I'm

all business with some of them, and I need to get to know more about their personal lives. But I'm worn out, and with my defenses down, I can't deny how much I miss my conversations with Ryan.

For weeks, I told myself it was over, once I knew RoughRider's identity. The magic was in the mystery. I couldn't confide my deepest feelings and desires in my brother's best friend, the man I'd known since he was a boy with scrawny arms and a crooked grin.

But I miss him. I don't just miss the anonymous RoughRider; I miss the man he truly is, which means I miss Ryan. I told myself I was *supposed* to deny it, but why? Ryan started seeing me differently ten years ago, and I unknowingly started seeing him differently as we exchanged messages.

There are men I could reach out to for a date, sex, or just conversation to get my mind off Ryan. I don't want to, though. There's only one man I want to talk to, and wondering if he misses me too is about to drive me over the edge.

Even though I know he hasn't messaged me, I open my Foxy app often, just to make sure. I open it for the second time today, sighing when I confirm he hasn't written.

I'm so focused on getting the New York office open that during the day, I don't have much time to think about where Ryan and I left things. But at night, even though I'm completely exhausted, I slip slowly into sleep, distracted by thoughts of him.

Does he check the Foxy app for no reason too? Is he trying to move on by dating someone? Does he *really* regret reaching out to me as RoughRider?

I guess he probably does. Like he said, he wants all or nothing, and our current relationship is more nothing than it's ever been. But now that I've had time to think about things, I'm glad he did it. Ryan has had feelings for me for ten years, and I had no idea. What if he'd never told me?

It's ridiculous for me to be sitting alone in this conference room, the unanswered questions still nagging at me. This is Ryan. I know him. I'm going to just ask him.

Before I can talk myself out of it, I message him.

SIENNAM: *I know you're teaching right now, but . . . hi.*

I'm surprised when he writes back quickly.

ROUGHRIDER16: *Hey. I'm teaching Driver's Ed this morning, and I'm in between students.*

SIENNAM: *Yikes, like the actual driving part?*

ROUGHRIDER16: *Yep. The kids are more scared about it than I am . . . usually.*

SIENNAM: *What's the 16 for in your screen name?*

ROUGHRIDER16: *My jersey number when I played football at Ohio State.*

SIENNAM: *Ah.*

ROUGHRIDER16: *Coop told me you're in NY. How's it going?*

SIENNAM: *Busy, but good.*

SIENNAM: *Do you miss our convos?*

ROUGHRIDER16: *Yes. Do you?*

SIENNAM: *Yes.*

ROUGHRIDER16: *Would they hold the same appeal now that you know it's me?*

SIENNAM: *Would I be bringing it up if not?*

ROUGHRIDER16: *idk, would you?*

SIENNAM: *I'm totally swamped with work, and I try to fill in the* gaps for Carmen with Jack as much as I can since Jack's dad is a deadbeat loser, so I don't have much of a social life.

ROUGHRIDER16: *Same here. I'm crazy busy with football season.*

SIENNAM: *Does that mean you don't have time for dating?*

ROUGHRIDER16: *Depends who's asking . . .*

SIENNAM: *I've been wondering if you're trying to move on by dating other women.*

ROUGHRIDER16: *No, not right now. You think I should?*

SIENNAM: *No.*

SIENNAM: *You hurt my feelings that night at my place.*

ROUGHRIDER16: *I've hurt over you for YEARS, babe. Call it even?*

SIENNAM: *Maybe . . .*

ROUGHRIDER16: *What do you want, Sienna? Don't play games with me.*

SIENNAM: *I honestly don't know. I guess what I'm saying is, if I had a different life . . . I'd want to date you. I've had time to get over the shock and see you in a different light. You're amazing.*

ROUGHRIDER16: *Coming from you, that's enough to sustain me for the next 20 years or so . . .*

SIENNAM: *Ryan Lennox, you have me on a pedestal. You'd be disappointed in the real deal. I'm a workaholic. I don't know how to cook. I haven't had a bikini wax in ages, and I kinda don't even care.*

ROUGHRIDER16: *You can be my sugar mama, I'll cook, and TRUST ME, I don't give a fuck about it.*

SIENNAM: *I'm going to be here for the next week, then I'll be in LA for a few days, then I need to be with Carmen and Jack. I truly don't* have time for even one date right now, but if I did . . . I'd want it to be with you.

RoughRider16: Why the change of heart?

SiennaM: It wasn't a change, really. I just needed time. And I still wouldn't be all in, like you want, but . . . I just wanted to tell you . . . I think about you, and I miss you.

RoughRider16: That means a lot to me. I miss you too. More than I can put into words.

SiennaM: I wish I could say let's take a shot when things change for me, but with the NY and LA offices in the works, and Jack . . .

RoughRider16: What's his prognosis?

SiennaM: He has a type of Batten's that makes it statistically impossible he'll see adulthood.

RoughRider16: Fucking hell. I didn't realize it was a certainty.

SiennaM: It is.

RoughRider16: I'm sorry, but my student just got here. Talk later?

SiennaM: Yes, this evening?

RoughRider16: Have practice and then reviewing film with my coaches. Would 9:30 work?

SiennaM: Maybe? That's 10:30 here, and I'm running on empty. If I don't message tonight, I will tomorrow.

RoughRider16: Get some sleep, Pup. I'm not going anywhere. And I'm not just talking about tonight.

The words "RoughRider16 has left the conversation" are blurred by welling tears when they appear on my screen.

I've been let down too many times to hope, and I have to stay sharply focused on the Alpha Mail expansion, but like I do with Jack, I let myself savor the moment of joy.

This moment feels good. Better than I've felt in a while, actually. I smile, dab at the corners of my eyes, and head into the conference room for lunch.

TWENTY-TWO

#mywholelifeinonelittlepackage

I TAKE IN a huge breath of muggy Chicago air as I step off my flight home. It may not smell pleasant, but it does smell like home. My trips back and forth between New York and LA have been ongoing for two weeks now, with no time for a stop home in between.

Opening two new offices at the same time was overly ambitious. I'm not sure I'll do it again. As soon as I get things rolling at one office, something inevitably comes up at the other one.

Things are good now, with the New York office officially open and the LA one opening soon. I'm finally comfortable going home and leaving things in the hands of my managers at each branch.

I couldn't be happier it's Friday night. I don't have to go into work tomorrow for the first time since I left Chicago. There was no reason to take weekends off in New York and LA. It's a little after 8:00 p.m., so I might be able to catch Jack before he goes to bed. I hope so. I missed him terribly.

After I see Jack, all I want to do is take a hot shower and change out of my comfy travel clothes—yoga pants and a T-shirt—into clean yoga pants and a T-shirt. Then I'm planning to talk to Carmen for a while, eat, and get an amazing night of sleep.

Ryan and I have been messaging off and on, but with my work schedule, it's been tough. What little extra time I have is mostly spent talking to Carmen. Jack has been forgetting things and losing his coordination more frequently. I know it's hard for her to talk about it because of what it means, but I also know that if she wants to talk about it, I need to drop everything and be there to listen.

One of my investors owns a car service, and I'm grateful she offered me free rides anytime I'm traveling. I'm so jet-lagged I don't even feel like driving, and it's nice to have the driver pile my bags into the trunk and deal with traffic while I zone out in the back seat.

I actually fall asleep on the twenty-five-minute trip to my place, and I wake up disoriented when the driver opens my door.

"Thank you," I murmur, handing him a tip.

He helps me in with my bags, and as soon as I close the door behind him, Carmen is standing in the living room. She's wringing a dishtowel in her hands, her cheeks streaked with tears.

"Oh my God, what is it?" I drop my bag and run toward her, my arms open.

My heart races with worry as she cries. After a few seconds, she pulls herself together and says, "Jack. He's getting confused and forgetting things . . ." She closes her eyes and sighs deeply. "And I keep it together in front of him, because I don't want him to know, but—"

"It's okay." I hold her tightly, my heart hurting for her. "I'm here now. You can let it all out to me."

She pulls back, gives me a sad smile, and swipes her fingertips beneath her eyes. "Thanks. But I need to figure out how to be honest about Jack's illness in front of him. I've been talking to my therapist about it, and I get why I've hidden it from him until now. I was in denial myself, and I wanted him to feel normal. But . . . he's terminally ill."

I shake my head, a lump burning my throat. "How do you make a six-year-old understand that?"

"I'm supposed to give him the answers he asks for, as gently as I can." She sits down on the couch, wringing the towel between her fingers again. "I just don't want to break down in front of him, even though my counselor says it's okay if I do. I want to be strong for him."

"I know." I sit down on the coffee table so I'm facing her. "But there's no right or wrong way to do this, Carmen. And as hard as it is to talk about, or even think about . . . there are things you should say to Jack while he can still understand them."

She sniffles, tears pooling in her eyes. "Should I tell him I'd give my life for him? Because I would. I ask God all the time why it's him and not me. I don't *want* to live without him, Sienna."

Her expression is pure agony. I ache for her. But she needs me to hold her up right now, not crumble.

"You should tell him he's the best thing that ever happened to you." My voice breaks as I say it. "Show him the photos of you holding him and tell him that was . . . the greatest day of your whole life."

When she closes her eyes, tears course down her cheeks. "It was."

"Tell him you'll love him for every second he's on this earth, and every second after. And that . . ." I take a breath, trying to compose myself. "That you never would have understood unconditional love without being his mom."

She nods. "I do need to tell him those things. I will."

"What can I do?" I reach out and put my palms on her knees. "Just tell me. Anything in the world."

"You're already doing it. Being able to spend every minute he's awake with him and not have to worry about money is the greatest gift anyone has ever given me, or ever will."

"I love you both," I say softly.

"And we love you." She pats one of my hands and then gestures at her wrist. "This thing is a lifesaver, you know."

"You like it?"

She glances at the rubber bracelet with a small monitor attached to it. It looks like a fitness tracker, but it's actually a device I had made for her. She attaches a monitor to Jack when he goes to bed, and the monitor on her wrist will buzz and sound an alarm if Jack's vital signs change.

"It's amazing. I can take showers. Long, hot, amazing showers. I was just in the kitchen baking completely by myself. Before, I felt like I needed to be at Jack's side every second, even when he was sleeping."

"I was hoping to catch him before he went to bed." I look over at the stairway, half hoping to see Jack peering at me through the rails, grinning.

"He was tired tonight. Long day."

"I'm sorry."

She gives me a half smile and says, "You know how they say when it rains it pours?"

I nod.

"Well, in addition to Jack having a really bad day today, I found out his dad is in prison. Danny is serving a seven-year term that started a year ago."

"Oh, shit. How'd you find out?"

"He emailed me asking for money."

I arch my brows. "I hope you told him to fuck off."

"I just deleted the email." She shrugs. "He doesn't even deserve acknowledgement. What I'm bummed about is that it means Jack will probably never see him again. And as stupid as this is, I really thought it was Danny who sent that Darth Vader and his team of Stormtroopers. For a stupid, crazy minute, I thought it might even *be* Danny in that suit."

I sit up on the coffee table, remembering the *Star Wars* flash mob in front of my house. "Well, if it wasn't Danny, then w—" I go completely still.

"What?"

"Team of Stormtroopers," I murmur. "Holy shit, Carmen."

"The way they all jogged away in formation like that, it was like—"

"It was like a football team. Because it *was* a football team."

"Ryan," she breathes.

"Ryan."

She breaks out in a slow, wide smile. "Sienna . . . that man is incredible. If you don't go to him *right now* and kiss the hell out of him, I'm going to kick your ass."

My heart flutters wildly. "Now? But it's late, and I don't know where he is, and I look like—" I glance down at my clothes "—hell. I look like hell. Maybe I should just—"

Carmen interjects, looking me square in eyes. "Are you wearing deodorant?"

"I put some on this morning."

"Then get your keys and go. I'll find out where Ryan is and text you."

I furrow my brow. "How can you find out?"

"Coop."

"Oh." I'll have to digest that bit of information later. "Okay."

"Go." She gets up and plucks her cell phone from a nearby end table.

"Okay." I stand up and run a hand over my hair, my blood pumping with excitement and affection for Ryan at the same time.

He was Darth Vader. I feel it in my heart without even getting his confirmation. The things he said to Jack, and the way the Stormtroopers stood in formation, jogging away on his command . . .

How did I not figure it out sooner? I guess, like Carmen, I wanted to believe it was Danny. But Ryan gave Jack a beautiful gift that day. He made him believe his father took the time to do something special for him.

Carmen is right. It doesn't matter what I look like right now. I grab my keys and bag, then scramble out the door.

By the time I've made it to my car, unlocked it and gotten inside, there's a message on my phone from Carmen.

CARMEN: *He's coaching a football game at Oakhurst High School. Got get him, girl.*

I punch the school's name into my GPS, take a deep breath, and start driving.

WHEN I WALK into the Oakhurst football stadium, I'm greeted by a sea of blue shirts and hats in the stands on the home field side. Based on the posters being waved in the air, the school mascot is an eagle.

Oakhurst is an upscale suburban school, and the stadium grounds are immaculate. The dark green field is wrapped by an enormous track, and the scent of popcorn and grilled pork chops fills the air.

I glance at the scoreboard and see that Ryan's team is up 27–7 in the fourth quarter. There are only two minutes left. Perfect.

My pulse is pounding as I walk over to the Eagles' sideline. When I see Ryan, my stomach flutters with nervous excitement. He's wearing a royal blue polo with his team's logo, his biceps and shoulders fully filling the sleeves, and a gray Eagles baseball hat.

He looks down at a clipboard, says something to an assistant coach, and then crosses his arms over his chest to pay attention to the game as it resumes.

I'm drawn to him, still approaching even though I can't talk to him during the game. That is, until a security guard steps into my path, shaking his head.

Damn. I'll have to settle for staring at Ryan's broad back while I wait, which is at least a nice view. When he turns to the side and I see his clean-shaven profile, it sets in for the first time how unbelievably handsome he is.

I knew he was attractive before, but right now, I can *feel* it. As my eyes slowly take in the lines of his body, I wonder how I ever could have been confused about my feelings for him. Am I in love with Ryan? At this moment, I can't honestly answer yes. But could I be, in time?

Hell yes. I've never wanted to dive headfirst off a cliff for any man the way I want to for Ryan right now.

The clock ticks down painfully slowly, stopping constantly just to taunt me. I tap my foot on the ground anxiously as I wait.

Finally, in the last minute of the game, the clock isn't stopping constantly anymore. Even with the game well in hand, Ryan is wearing a serious expression, nodding solemnly at something a player says to him.

When it ends, the crowd erupts in cheers, and my heart rate accelerates as I run toward the field. I call out his name as I get closer, but he can't hear me over the sounds of celebration.

He's smiling his satisfied grin, his brown eyes sparkling. God, he looks good. I yell his name at the top of my lungs as I rush forward, and he turns.

I'm breathless as I cover the last twenty feet separating us, and when I reach him, his eyes widen with surprise.

"What are you doing here?"

I'm still breathing heavily as I say, "You're Darth Vader, aren't you?"

His grin fades, and he looks away. "I didn't do it to impress you."

"How did you know?" I put a hand on his wrist, needing to feel him. "How did you know that Jack loves *Star Wars* and his dad hasn't been around?"

"Coop told me his dad's a deadbeat a while back. I stopped by your parents' place to pick up some stuff they were donating for a fundraiser at the school, and your mom told me the rest."

"So you did that *Star Wars* thing just for Jack? Did Coop know?"

Ryan shakes his head. "No one knew but me and . . ." He gestures to the group of players jumping up and down in a huddle behind him.

"The Stormtroopers."

He nods. "I didn't want anyone to know either. It wasn't about you, Sienna. I don't want you to think I was trying to—"

I interrupt him. "Ask me out."

He cocks a brow in surprise.

"Ask me," I repeat.

"I didn't do it so you'd go out with me."

"And I don't want to go out with you because you did it."

He gives me a skeptical look. "Then why are you telling me to ask you out right after you figured it out?"

"Ryan Lennox." My voice is louder than I intended. "Ask me out. You said you love me."

A few players turn in our direction.

"I do love you. But *you* said you don't have time for even one single date. The only thing that's changed since then is you finding out about the *Star Wars* thing."

Tears of frustration sting my eyes. "So, you won't do it, then?"

He moves his hand so my palm slides from his wrist and into his gentle grip. "I want more than just a date, Pup." His dark caramel eyes hold me in a trance.

"I do too. But we have to start there, don't we?"

More people are listening to us now, but Ryan doesn't seem to see anyone but me.

"You're sure you want this? Because once I have you . . . I'm not letting go."

"I'm sorry it took me so long to figure it out, but I do. I want this." My heart pounds against my ribcage as he holds my gaze for a full second.

Then, he sweeps me off my feet in an embrace that takes my breath away. His players cheer as he spins me in a circle and then sets me down.

"Will you go out with me?" he asks softly as he looks down at me.

"I thought you'd never ask."

I cup his cheeks, lean forward, and kiss him. He tastes like cinnamon, and his stubble scrapes against my lips as he bends and wraps me into his arms again, dropping his clipboard and deepening the kiss.

People from the stands are cheering now too. I laugh lightly as Ryan pulls back for just a second and then kisses me again. He's all warmth, solid strength, and longing. Nothing has ever felt as good as this.

I don't feel hope or regret right now. I'm not looking forward or backward. It's just a moment of pure joy I let fill me from head to toe, and it's utterly perfect.

TWENTY-THREE

#datenight

A FLUSH CREEPS up my neck to my cheeks as I admire the black dress and heels I'm wearing in the mirror. The dress has a slightly conservative cut, but it hugs me well in all the right places. And the leopard print heels were a splurge just for this date.

It's not just the clothes themselves making me feel warm and excited, but knowing I'm wearing them for Ryan. He insisted on taking me to a nice restaurant tonight, even though I told him I'd be fine with pizza or burgers.

I'd be okay with anything as long as it's with him. Now that I've come to my senses, I'm making up for all the years of not seeing Ryan as the sexy, smart, big-hearted catch he really is. I daydream about him at work and end every night on the phone with him, sighing softly and smiling when we hang up.

"You look amazing," Carmen says as I walk downstairs.

"Thanks."

Jack is curled up on the couch, his head in her lap and a *Star Wars* blanket tucked around him. He smiles at me, but he doesn't say anything. He's been quieter lately, likely because he can't find the words for what he wants to say, or because he's not even sure what to say.

It's a cruel disease he's been stricken with, but Carmen insists that we all keep living life even though he's sick. She still wants him to be a little boy as much as he possibly can. Tonight, they're having a *Star Wars* and pizza night, with cupcakes cooling in the kitchen to frost and decorate later.

The doorbell rings, and I race over to answer the door. Ryan stands before me in a pale blue button-up shirt, tailored dark gray pants, and shining black shoes. He takes me in with a slow, sexy smile.

"You're beautiful," he says, meeting my eyes.

"Thank you." I smile nervously. "You're early."

He shrugs a shoulder. "Couldn't help myself. Besides, a true alpha never picks his woman up late."

Warmth at the sound of him calling me his woman swirls in my belly. "Is that so?"

He nods, a corner of his mouth turning up in a smile. I step aside, and he comes in to say hi to Carmen and Jack. When Jack sees him, he sits up, his expression bright.

"The locks still work," he tells Ryan with a smile.

"Great. Thanks for keeping an eye on them for me."

Jack snuggles against Carmen's side contentedly. Carmen meets my eyes with a small smile, silently wishing me good luck.

"Ready?" I ask Ryan.

"Whenever you are."

True to his word, he opens the door for me, stepping aside so I can walk through first. He offers me a hand as we descend the stairs down to the sidewalk, and I take it.

"How was your Saturday?" he asks as he leads the way to his truck.

"It was really good. We went to the farmers market this

morning and then had lunch with my parents downtown since they're visiting. How about you?"

"The team did a project for an elderly couple in town, so I helped with that. We did yard work and painting."

When we get to his truck, he opens the door for me. I should get in, but instead, I just look at him. I've always known in the back of my mind that he was handsome, but now I'm starting to see him in a new light. He's not just Coop's good-looking friend anymore. He's Ryan. My RoughRider. And that man gives me the weak-in-the-knees, giddy sense of hopefulness I haven't let myself feel in years.

Ryan lets me look without asking me if something's wrong. He knows why I'm looking, and he looks back, a smile playing on his lips.

I reach for him, pressing myself against his chest and wrapping my arms around his neck. He encircles his strong arms around my back, making me feel warm and secure.

If only this moment could last forever. I'm so content that I moan softly and press a soft kiss to his neck. He responds with a sound deep in his throat that sounds like a growl.

"You really are an alpha, aren't you?" I say in his ear.

He lets out a deep, soft laugh and rests his forehead against mine. "With you, I am."

"I kind of don't want to move and get in the truck," I admit.

Ryan pulls back slightly and gives me an amused grin. "I kind of don't want you to either, but we've got a reservation."

I slide my hands out from around his neck and down his chest, reveling in the hard, solid feel of him. The thought of feeling his bare skin sends a shiver of desire from the tip of my spine to the base.

Ryan's eyes slide closed for just a second. I love that he likes my hands on him. But he's right, we have dinner plans, and I want to enjoy the date he planned for us.

When I step up into his truck, he offers me a hand for support. Once I'm in, he closes the door, and I laugh to myself as he walks around the truck to get inside. I feel like a high school girl again, wishing he would park the truck somewhere so we could just make out all night.

He takes me to a little basement-level restaurant in the city called Leonardo's. It's dimly lit, the walls covered with photos of the owner and all the famous people who have eaten here over the years. The air is filled with the scent of garlic and authentic Italian music piped through speakers.

"This place has the best lasagna," he murmurs as we're led to our table. "Ever been here?"

"No, but it's great. Just perfect."

Over dinner, he tells me about his team and the classes he teaches. He has a passion for history that I never saw in him. His deepest passion is football, though. I like the way he talks about his team as a whole, but also sees each player as an individual.

"I guess I'm kind of a hard-ass," he says with a wry smile. "I never thought I would be. When I was a player, I swore I'd be the coolest coach ever."

"You have to be pretty hard if you want to have a winning team."

He nods. "And the funny thing is, the boys respond well to it. I don't just want to coach them in the game of football, but in life. We talk about how to treat people and look out for yourself and all that too."

"You're probably the only father figure some of them have," I say, thinking of Jack.

Ryan reaches across the table and takes my hand. He rubs his thumb over my knuckles, his gaze intently focused on me.

He's not nervous. At all. I'm the only one whose insides feel like they're on spin cycle right now. Ryan seems to know, with crystal clarity, that all he needed was a chance with me. And damn, does his confidence turn me on like nothing else.

"I'm sorry it took me time to get here," I say softly.

"We're here. That's all that matters."

The lasagna really is amazing, and we eat slowly as Ryan listens to me go on and on about the Alpha Mail expansion and Carmen and Jack. After dinner, we walk downtown, meandering past shop windows hand in hand as we continue talking. We stop at a small ice cream parlor, where I get a cookies and cream waffle cone and he gets a strawberry one.

It's a little after ten when we get back to his car, and I'm hoping he plans to take me back to his place. After this evening of being so physically close to him, I want him in ways I never thought possible. I love his light, masculine scent that reminds me of cedar. I'm driven mad by the way he looks at me, a fire in his eyes that he keeps reined in.

I want him to unleash that fire and have his way with me until sunrise. This date has only confirmed what I already suspected—I'm falling hard for Ryan.

He drives back to my place, though, so I invite him in as he walks me up the stairs to the front door.

"I'd love to, but I think I shouldn't," he says with a grin.

"Really?" My disappointment is obvious.

Ryan's expression turns serious as he cups my cheeks in his hands. "I'm not doing a single thing to mess this up. The reason I'm not coming in isn't because I don't want you really fucking bad . . . it's because I do."

I nod, so warm I wouldn't feel a blizzard passing by right now.

He runs a thumb over my cheekbone and says, "I want to see

you again as soon as possible. I can do almost anytime but Friday nights during the season."

"Yes. And . . . maybe Carmen and Jack and I can come to one of your games?"

"I'd love that."

I sigh softly. "So no crazy alpha sex for me tonight, then."

Ryan groans and kisses my forehead. "We'll get there. And when we do, it won't just be sex."

He kisses me then, and it's only slow and sweet for a couple seconds. Then he pulls me against him, one of his hands on my waist, as his kiss becomes deeper, more insistent. When his hand slides down to cup my ass, he seems to catch himself, pulling away.

"I have to go," he whispers against my lips. "You make it hard to be a gentleman."

I just nod, breathless. I'm pretty sure I manage to say goodnight before I float into the house and close the door, leaning my back against it as I close my eyes and smile.

Every horrible date was worth it. It was those dates that led me here, and there's nowhere else I'd rather be.

TWENTY-FOUR

#thestrongone

ISAAC HASN'T STOPPED smiling since he walked in the room almost an hour ago. He seems truly touched by the going-away party we surprised him with.

Jane had lunch and an amazing cake catered in, and I gave Isaac an Apple watch, his going-away present from the Chicago office. Lucky for us, he isn't going completely away—he's just transferring to the New York office. He's keeping his client roster, so it'll be business as usual from a new location.

After the stalking thing, Isaac decided he needed a change of scenery. He's officially moving this weekend. I'll be glad to have a veteran employee in the new office.

"Thanks for everything, Sienna." He offers me a hand, but I hug him instead.

"You'll still be seeing plenty of me."

The party starts breaking up, and Jane begins sweeping in for cleanup duty. I help her get the conference room back in order, and then I go back to my office.

The first thing I do is look at my phone, and the second thing I do is smile when I see messages waiting on my Foxy app.

ROUGHRIDER16: *Hey, gorgeous. How's your day?*

ROUGHRIDER16: *Mine's been decent, other than a near-death experience when a kid mistook the brake pedal for the gas pedal in driver's ed this morning . . .*

ROUGHRIDER16: *I couldn't even be mad at him, because he peed his pants. Not like fully soaked, but enough to cause embarrassment.*

ROUGHRIDER16: *But seriously, if I hadn't gone to the bathroom before we left, I may have pissed myself too. He floored it across an intersection with a semi coming from the other direction.*

I can just picture Ryan, outwardly cool and collected, but inwardly shaken by the oncoming semi. I write him back.

SIENNAM: *I don't know how you do it. I'd be yelling at those kids to get out of the car and let me drive . . .*

SIENNAM: *Good day here. Any day with cake is good.*

SIENNAM: *NY office is exceeding all projections. Couldn't be happier about it.*

SIENNAM: *Also, I get to see you in two days! I miss you.*

We have each other's cell numbers, but we keep using the Foxy app for old times' sake. I like seeing "RoughRider16" on the screen and knowing it's Ryan on the other end.

I've cut back on my work schedule, taking weekends completely off and leaving the office by five every day. With Jack declining, I want to be home with him and Carmen every evening. Even though I know she can do it all on her own, I see the relief in her eyes when I walk in each night. When I'm with Jack, she feels comfortable taking a little quiet time for herself with a book or calling a friend to catch up.

Ryan's team has an away game this week, but we're planning to go to next week's home game. On Friday night, Jack and I bake cookies and listen to a radio broadcast of Ryan's team playing.

"I . . . can't," Jack says as he tries to grab the spoon in the bowl of dough to stir it.

"Want some help?" I offer.

He nods, looking deflated. It's hard seeing him not be able to do things he used to have no trouble with. I help him get the spoon into his hand and stir the dough, and then we work together to shape the dough for baking.

When our cookies are done, Jack takes several and sits in my lap to nibble on them. I close my eyes and soak in his sweet, warm presence. Eventually, we both fall asleep coated in cookie crumbs.

The next day is Saturday—date night with Ryan. And even though I'm pretty sure he still won't give in and ravage me all night long, I'm hoping to at least get in a long make-out session.

It's fall now, so I wear black leather leggings with strappy black booties and a slinky little purple top. If Ryan won't fuck me senseless just yet, might as well try to drive him crazy anyway.

I get a hungry once-over from him, and an approving nod, when he picks me up. Once we're inside his truck, he puts his hand on my thigh and gives a low groan.

"Leather," he says in a low tone. "Damn, Sienna."

"If you think the leather feels good, wait till you feel what's beneath it."

Ryan inhales deeply, gathering himself, and then turns to me, cupping my cheek and drawing us together for a kiss. His mouth is warm and demanding, the scrape of his stubble against my lips making me moan softly.

He pulls back slightly. "I want you, but that's nothing new for me. I've wanted you for ten fucking years, Pup. And you wanting me back feels so damn amazing. But we're waiting until I know you're ready for it."

I arch a brow, amused. "Don't I get to decide when I'm ready for it?"

"No. You have no idea what you're in for. You think you can have a casual night of sex with a two-hundred-pound man who's deeply in love and sexually starved? Who takes out all those frustrations in the gym? You'll never be the same after our first time, and I won't be either."

Desire ripples down my spine, heating my core and leaving me breathless. Ryan Lennox has never been all talk. I feel the intensity and sincerity of his words down to my bones.

"When . . ." My voice breaks nervously, and I clear my throat. "Um . . . when do you think I might be ready, then?"

His lips curve up in a small smile. "Soon. But not tonight."

I have a sudden longing I can't help blurting out. "Tell me you love me, Ryan."

He holds my gaze and says, "I love you. Always have and always will, babe."

My stomach flutters with nervous excitement. There's nothing like his dark chocolate eyes on me as he says the words that have come to mean everything to me.

Ryan loves me. I'm falling hard for him. And there's no reason to rush. It's actually kind of beautiful to savor this part.

We start our evening at Lucky Seven. I've spent many hours at this bar with Coop and Ryan, but that was before RoughRider rode into my life. I like how it feels to walk in with him holding my hand.

Coop is actually here tonight, and he gives our linked hands a long look before grinning and inviting us to sit down. When he hugs me, he murmurs, "He treating you okay?" in my ear, and I tell him yes.

"How's Jack doing?" Coop asks me, his expression solemn.

"As expected. He's having trouble with motor skills and memory. It's heartbreaking."

"Anything I can do?"

"Maybe come by and see him. He'd like that."

Coop nods. "I will. I'd like that too."

"I guess you and Carmen can work it out since you have each other's numbers and all." I give him a knowing look.

He looks like the cat that swallowed the canary as he says, "I guess we can."

Ryan gives me a questioning look, and I silently tell him I'll explain later.

"You guys want to get pizza?" Coop asks. "I'm starving."

"Yeah." I look at Ryan. "Yeah? Is that good with you?"

"I was planning to just grab a drink here and take you somewhere nicer for dinner, but if you're okay with pizza, I'm good with it."

I snuggle against his side. "I'm good with pizza. Let's stay."

"I see who's running this relationship," Coop says with a laugh.

"We're co-running it." I frown at him.

"Yeah, you keep telling yourself that."

"Outside the bedroom, she can run anything she wants," Ryan says.

Coop's amused grin disappears. "Let's not go there. That's my sister you're talking about."

We order a pitcher of beer and two large pizzas, catching up as we wait for the food. It feels so good—like old times, but better. As we tell funny stories from childhood, I think about something Ryan said to me recently. No man will ever know me like he does. He's right. And no woman could ever know him like I do. That added intimacy makes me want him—all of him—even more.

I keep my hand on Ryan's leg beneath the table, enjoying the effect I can have on him. When I slide my palm higher, I get a sharp intake of breath and a tightening of his muscles. I can feel him relax as I move my hand lower, and then I slowly repeat the process.

Our pizzas are delivered, and we're about to start eating when my phone rings from inside my purse. When I look at the screen and see Carmen's name, my heart hammers nervously.

"Carmen?"

There's a couple seconds of silence before she says, "Sienna, I need you."

Her voice is strained with emotion. I stand up from my chair and say, "Where?"

"CMC. We're on the way to the ER. Jack's having a seizure."

I grab on to Ryan's arm for support. "I'm on my way."

Ryan's standing now too. "Jack?"

I nod, my breathing shallow as I process what's happening. "I need to get to the CMC ER. Right now."

"Let's go." Ryan takes my hand.

Coop throws some bills onto our table and runs after us.

IT'S BEEN THE longest three hours of my life. I'm sitting in the Chicago Medical Center ER waiting area, elbows on my knees, looking at the ground. Ryan's beside me, his arm around my shoulders. Coop is on the other side, switching between pacing nervously and sulking in his chair.

I'm not family, the receptionist said, so I'm not allowed inside. It felt like a slap in the face, because Carmen and Jack *are* family in my heart, and she has no one else. I'm crying slow, silent tears that drip onto the worn linoleum floor at my feet, not only for Jack, but for Carmen, who is probably out of her mind with worry and helplessness.

"I have to keep it together for her," I murmur, turning my face just slightly toward Ryan.

"You will." He runs his hand down to my back and pulls me against him. "You can come apart later, with me."

I reach for his free hand and squeeze it in mine, another silent tear sliding down my cheek.

"There she is," Coop says, bounding out of his chair.

I sit up and see Carmen approaching us, her eyes raw and swollen. I can't get to her fast enough.

Coop beats me, folding her into his arms, where she cries harder than I've ever seen her cry. He closes his eyes and rests his cheek on top of her head, his expression more wrecked than I've ever seen it.

Finally, she pulls away, giving Coop a sad smile as she wipes her cheeks.

"He's stable," she says, looking from Coop to me.

Ryan's behind me now, his hands on my shoulders.

I reach for Carmen's hand, questions pouring out of me. "Will he be okay? Is he in pain? Can I come back there with you and see him?"

She squares her shoulders. "This is part of the progression of Batten's. The doctors won't know how much it affected his brain until some more testing is done. He's not in pain. They've taken really good care of him. We're staying tonight, and you can come back with me now."

"Can I stay too?"

She shrugs. "I don't know . . . I'll ask. But you don't have to."

"I want to."

"I know." Her eyes flood with grateful tears. "But I won't be able to sleep at all tonight, and it's going to catch up with me eventually. If I have to sleep, I want to know you're with him. So can you try to sleep tonight?"

"Of course. Anything you need."

Her tears spill over then, and I reach for her, hugging her tightly. I wish I had words that would comfort her, but I don't. This is the ugly reality of Jack's disease, and there's no soothing the heart of a mother watching her child suffer.

All I can do is be here, and I will. For every brutal, crushing step of the way, I'll be here.

TWENTY-FIVE

#nohedidnt

I SCAN THE sidelines, warming when my gaze lands on Ryan's broad shoulders. He's wearing a gray polo and blue baseball hat tonight, talking into his headset.

It's been a hell of a week, and just seeing Ryan grounds me. When Jack woke up at the hospital, he was still himself, which left me so relieved I went into the bathroom and cried for five minutes.

But in the days after that, Carmen and I realized that while the seizure didn't give him long-term physical or mental damage, it absolutely did change him. He's scared now, the memory of the seizure and its aftermath haunting him. After Carmen and a pediatrician told him what's happening with the progression of his disease, the light went out of him.

This is what Carmen wanted to put off as long as possible. Jack knows he's only going to get worse from here. His dream of playing with the neighborhood kids seems insignificant compared to his new dream of surviving.

We've got a system now. I've been working from home and taking care of Jack during the day, with the help of a home health nurse, while Carmen sleeps for a few hours. She seems to feel guilty every time she sleeps. She sits with Jack at night, reading to him and watching him sleep, keeping vigil in case he has another seizure.

Next week, we're changing our routine. I hired a second nurse to monitor Jack overnight. I hope it will help Carmen sleep at night, so she can be with Jack during the day, with help from the other nurse.

We hadn't been out of the house all week, and Jack wanted to come to Ryan's game like we'd planned. Carmen immediately said yes, because Jack hasn't asked for much since coming home from the hospital.

So here we are, bundled in blankets, dressed in blue, cheering on Ryan's team. None of us knows a lot about football, but we know how to join in when the home team is cheering.

"I'm glad we came," I say to Carmen over Jack's head during a semi-quiet moment.

"Me too."

Jack is snuggled between us, sipping hot chocolate and watching the game intently. I'm trying to watch the game, but I keep finding myself distracted by Ryan. I like seeing him standing on the sidelines, watching and directing his players. The other team's coach is waving his arms all over the place, yelling and looking like a heart attack about to happen. Ryan is cool, collected, and focused.

The game is tied 7–7 when one of Ryan's players intercepts the ball. I'm cheering along with everyone else as he runs, when suddenly Jack jumps up off the bleachers.

He's making a frustrated sound that's not quite a word, over and over. Tears are streaming down his cheeks. Carmen and I both see the reason at the same time—he spilled the huge cup of hot chocolate all over his lap, and he's soaking wet.

"It's okay, baby," Carmen says.

Jack wails louder—probably both frustrated that he dropped

the cup *and* uncomfortable from the hot liquid on his skin.

"I shouldn't have gotten you that big cup." Carmen's trying to soothe Jack, and people are turning to look at us now.

"Hey," a woman in front of us says as she turns around. "Need a towel?"

I take it and give her a grateful look. "Thank you so much."

"No problem."

"I'm sorry if any of that got on you," I tell her, unfolding the towel and using it to dry Jack's clothes off a little.

She waves a hand. "I'm a mom. Stuff happens." She gives Jack an encouraging smile. "You okay, buddy? I've got some juice boxes if you want one."

People are still looking at us, and Jack gives Carmen a pained look. He's embarrassed, of course.

"I think we should go," Carmen murmurs.

"Sure." I start packing stuff up, and we all stand up to exit the row of bleachers.

"Cup!" Jack cries, pointing at the abandoned Styrofoam cup on the ground.

"It's empty, sweets," Carmen says.

"Cup!"

I bend down to get the cup and hand it to him, then return the towel to the woman in front of us and thank her again. I'm shuffling along next to Jack when I hear a deep bellow from behind us.

"Hey, get that retarded kid out of here!"

For one full second, I go still with shock. Now everyone in our section is either looking at us or at the balding, scowling guy in a blue T-shirt who yelled.

Jack's face is a deep shade of crimson, and so is Carmen's. I know for sure it's mortification on Jack's part and red-hot anger on Carmen's.

"You guys go," I say to Carmen when we get to the end of the row. "I'll meet you in the car."

"Sienna, he's not worth it."

"Just go," I say in a level tone.

My anger is of the white-hot variety. That asshole has no idea who he just crossed.

As Carmen takes Jack's hand and leads him down the concrete stadium stairs, I walk up them until I get to the row where the bearded man with a huge mouth is sitting. He gapes at me as if to say, "What?"

"Pretty tough of you to mouth off to a six-year-old." I hold his dark, beady-eyed gaze. "How about someone who's not terminally ill and not afraid of you? You got anything to say to me?"

He laughs. Laughs, and my blood boils.

"Get the fuck out of here, Red. I'm tryin' to watch the game."

"He's a *person*." My voice rises with emotion. "And you're an insensitive jerk."

The woman next to him sneers, her eyes widening like I'm in for it now.

"Okay, bitch, you want problems? You got 'em now."

The burly guy shuffles toward me, and all eyes are on us now. I refuse to move. If this fat lumberjack wants to fight me, I'm in. I don't care if he kicks my ass. The look he put on Jack's face has me ready to do battle.

Before the man can get to me, another man nearby stands up and blocks his path.

"Go sit down, Buck," he says.

"Oh, it's Buck, is it?" I lean around the man in front of me. "How fitting. Bet you've got more guns than teeth, am I right?"

The man turns around and gives me a wry smile. "Cool it, hotshot. Buck's an asshole, but we're in the middle of a high school football game."

A uniformed security guard shows up then, taking me by the arm and hauling me down the stadium stairs. I return every dirty look I get from onlookers. What kind of people just stand by and let someone treat a kid that way? I would have stood up whether it was Jack or a kid I didn't even know.

The game is in a time-out, and I find Ryan on the sidelines, gesturing at a clipboard and talking to several players. He looks up, sees me, and frowns.

Oh God. I didn't mean to interrupt his coaching. He passes off the clipboard to another coach and starts coming toward me.

The security guard tightens his hold on my arm, probably enjoying the looks we're getting as he drags me toward the stadium exit.

"Get your hands off her." Ryan's voice reaches us before he does.

The guard gives me a startled look, dropping his hand away.

"What are you doing?" Ryan demands, giving the guard a challenging look.

By his tone, it's clear he's pissed. I'm not sure I've ever seen Ryan so angry.

"She was causing a scene, Coach," the guard says apologetically.

Ryan looks at me, and I shrug unapologetically. "Some guy named Buck called Jack retarded."

The guard gives me a sheepish look. "I should probably make Buck leave too."

"You think?" Ryan's tone is clipped. He turns to me. "Are you okay?"

I nod. "I'm so sorry."

"Don't apologize. You didn't do anything wrong."

"Get back to your game. We can talk later."

"I'll deal with Buck after the game."

My eyes widen with horror. "Ryan, don't get yourself in trouble over this. This is your job."

He gives my shoulder a gentle squeeze. "Don't worry about it. We're not gonna tolerate that kind of behavior here."

I sigh softly. "I'm leaving because Jack spilled hot chocolate on himself, and . . . well, I got kicked out, so . . . yeah, I'm leaving."

"I'll call you as soon as I can." He squeezes my shoulder. "Love you."

I give him a grateful look. "Go win your game."

He smiles, then turns and jogs back to his team. And I realize that whether it's been long enough or we've gotten to see enough of each other's bad sides yet, I love him too. The same way he loves me—unequivocally.

TWENTY-SIX

#dontletgo

A YOUNG BLOND woman with a frazzled expression gives me a disapproving look the moment she spots me in the hallway of the New York Alpha Mail office.

"Ma'am, if you aren't an employee, you can't be in this area." She puts a foot in my path to stop me.

Am I more aggravated that she stopped me so rudely, or that she called me *ma'am*? Too close to call.

I smile, keeping my cool. "I'm pretty sure I'm authorized. I'm Sienna Mills."

"Oh." She puts a hand over her eyes, her cheeks flushing. "I'm so sorry."

"It's okay. They're hiring people so quickly here that I haven't met everyone yet. I've been away for two weeks."

"Yeah, I just started Monday. I'm Tori." She offers me a hand, and I shake it.

My smile is tighter this time. One of my pet peeves is people who only introduce themselves with their first name. I'm tired and stressed, though, so I brush it off.

"Tori . . . ?"

"Oh." She grins at me. "Tori Stanton. I'm one of the front desk receptionists."

"Well, it's great to meet you."

Two men are coming down the hallway from the other direction, one practically running. When I look at their faces, I recognize one of them as Isaac.

"Hey," he says quickly. "It's good you're here. This place is a zoo."

"Really?" I say a quick goodbye to Tori and fall in beside him.

"The management team is trying to keep up with demand, but it's overwhelming. No one has time for lunch, and we're all here late every night."

I suppress a sigh. "Why is this the first I'm hearing about this? That's not the way to keep good employees."

Isaac shrugs. "We're all getting overtime for it." He stops by an office door. "I have to go. I'm actually double-booked in five minutes."

"Double-booked? How does that work?"

He gives me a sheepish grin. "I talk to one client while texting another."

I cringe. "I don't love that, Isaac."

"I know." He puts his hands up. "But the phone call will be less than five minutes. I'm a pro, Sienna, you know that."

"And so modest." I give him a mock glare.

"Always."

"Let's talk more when you have time."

He laughs. "You can catch me when I'm walking to the bathroom, maybe? Other than that, there is no time."

"Shit." I wave at him and head for my office.

Good thing I listened to my intuition and came here. Even though the New York office is booming financially, I need it to run smoothly. We'll hire more people, stop taking clients—whatever it takes to get things on track.

It was so hard to leave home and come here, not knowing when I'll be able to return. Jack has been having seizures every day or two, and Carmen is barely holding it together. I hired home nurses to work all three shifts and also brought in someone to do the cooking and cleaning. At least I know Carmen has help, but I'm worried about her not having emotional support. Coop told me he'll stop by often to check on her, which is something.

I'm going to work hard to get things fixed here so I can get home. The New York management team better not complain about long hours while I'm here, because they got us into this mess.

When I take out my phone to check email, there's a waiting message on my screen.

RoughRider16: *Hey, did you make it okay?*

Crap. I forgot to let Ryan know I landed safely. I'm rusty on relationship protocol.

SiennaM: *Yes. It's a mess here. Miss you.*

RoughRider16: *Me too. Hurry home.*

I bypass my own office, instead walking into the office of my New York branch manager. Her day is probably crazy already, and it's about to get worse.

TWO WEEKS LATER, I have a newfound respect for Carmen. How she gets by on so little sleep, and still manages to smile, is beyond me.

I've been putting in days that start at sunrise and end around midnight. My first move was to demote my branch manager and bring in someone new. That took several days of calling contacts for recommendations and interviewing candidates.

At the same time, I was running the office myself. I quickly realized the New York manager needs not just one, but two assistants, and I started the hiring process for that.

I Skype with Carmen and Jack every day while I eat lunch, which is usually only a fifteen-minute break. Seeing their faces on the screen grounds me and reminds me why I'm here. Carmen tells me the nurses are taking good care of Jack, which is good, but every time Jack tells me he misses me and reaches toward the screen, it guts me.

I'd give anything to hug that kid, I sometimes think in the middle of another grueling workday.

By the time I'm done every night, I drop onto my office couch, too exhausted for more than a quick text to Ryan. We haven't talked at all in the past two weeks, and in the moments I have to think about something other than work, I miss him so much it hurts.

I miss his smile. His voice. His messages. His smell. All of it feels so far away right now.

It's Wednesday, and I'm helping with interviews for new alphas. I came back to my hotel for a quick shower, because I didn't feel like my deodorant could work the miracles I was asking of it any longer.

After drying my hair and putting on fresh makeup, I take the first clothes from my dry-cleaning stack and put them on. When I catch a look at the time in my peripheral vision, I do the conversion and realize it's a little after 6:00 p.m. back home. I planned this shower around the hope that I could talk to Ryan.

I call him, closing my eyes and saying a prayer he'll answer.

"Hey," he says, sounding out of breath. "How are you?"

"I miss you. So much."

"Me too, babe."

The sound of his deep, warm voice is like a caress for my worn nerves. "Did I catch you at an okay time?"

"Of course. One sec."

He must be covering the phone, because there's a muffled yelling sound on the other end of the line.

He returns and says, "Sorry about that."

"It's okay. Are you sure you can talk?"

"Yeah, I'm just at practice."

I close my eyes. "Of course you are. I'm sorry, I didn't mean to interrupt."

"Hey, stop. I haven't heard your voice in forever. Talk to me."

A smile tugs up the corners of my lips as I lean against the desk in my room. "I'm hoping to be done here soon. Things are finally shaping up."

"Good. I was pricing flights to come there this weekend."

"Ryan! It costs a fortune to fly last minute."

He laughs. "Yeah, and I could only come from Saturday to Sunday. And I know you're working weekends. I was gonna be your coffee boy, just so I could lay eyes on you."

"Just eyes?"

His low groan sends a shiver of longing throughout my body. "You want me to come? I will."

"Uh . . . do I . . . what?"

"To New York, babe."

"Oh, that." I laugh nervously. "I'd love it, but honestly, I'm working like eighteen hours a day."

Ryan hums his concern. "You have to be totally exhausted."

"Oh, I am. I fell asleep peeing the other day."

"Sienna . . ."

"I know. But this is me, Ryan. I work hard."

"Yeah, but you need time for yourself, and for the people who love you."

Something in his tone hits a nerve, and I fire back. "I'm *here* for the people who love me, Ryan. I know I'm not an ideal girlfriend right now, but I told you—"

Ryan cuts in. "Whoa. This isn't what I meant, okay?"

"Well, the guilt was already there, I guess. I'm not with Carmen and Jack, and he's getting worse every day. I'm not with you, and we just started dating like five minutes ago. The only thing I'm doing well right now is work."

"Sienna. Take a deep breath. It's okay."

I plow ahead, *not* taking a breath. "The money I'm making will pay for the care he's going to need. I never used to talk to Carmen about this stuff, because she enjoys every day she has with Jack and doesn't think about the future. And I get that, I do, but . . . I've researched, and eventually, he's going to need a feeding tube. He'll just keep declining and . . ." The lump in my throat burns.

"It's all right, babe," Ryan soothes me in a deep, gentle tone. "Just cry. You can always cry with me."

I breathe out, my shoulders sinking as tears slide down my cheeks. It's not just a few—within seconds, I'm sobbing, letting go of the control I had a tenuous grip on all day at work.

"I'm so torn," I finally say, still crying. "I want to be there with them. She needs me. But I have to be here, making sure this new location is doing well. The money matters, and I don't want Carmen to have to worry about it."

"You're doing everything you can. Carmen and Jack know you love them, Sienna. Don't let guilt take you down right now."

"It's so hard." My voice shakes, tears threatening to spill over again.

"It's one of the hardest fucking things anyone will ever go through," Ryan agrees. "And I love you for your strength, but you don't have to be strong around me."

"Ryan." I sit down on the edge of the bed, grabbing a tissue to mop the smeared mascara from my cheeks. "I've been thinking all afternoon about this conversation. Telling myself I could hold it together until I heard your voice."

He sighs softly into the phone. "I wish I were there, babe. More than you know."

"I feel like we're on the edge of something. Something amazing. But my life got turned upside down, and there's not even enough of me for Carmen, Jack, and my work. I don't have the emotional space to give you what you deserve right now."

I'm sobbing again, the unfairness of it all crushing me, making it hard to even take a breath.

"Sienna," Ryan says softly. "Do you want me in your life?"

"Yes. So much. It's like I'm drowning, and you're the only thing I have to hold on to and maybe have a shot at surviving." My voice breaks with emotion, high and strained.

"Then hold on to me. And I'll hold on to you too. I'll . . ." His voice breaks the same way mine did, because he's crying too. He clears his throat and continues. "I'll never let go. I know this isn't like the start of other relationships, but the way you're there for Jack and Carmen is one of the reasons I'm so in love with you. I'm all in, babe. Whatever you need from me, it's yours."

I sigh softly and close my eyes. "I love you, Ryan. I wanted to tell you in person, but—"

"Say it again."

"I love you."

"Goddamn, that feels good."

I sniffle, weak with relaxation now that my tension is finally released. "Thank you for . . . being you. And for loving me and not giving up on me. I never thought I'd have this."

"Me either. For you to let go like this, with me . . . you're letting me be what I always wanted to be for you."

"I can't wait to see you again."

"Me either."

"So . . ." I try to sound nonchalant, but fail. "How much longer on the whole goodnight kiss only thing?"

Ryan laughs. "You're wanting more, huh?"

"For fuck's sake, yes. If we love each other, don't you think we should . . . you know?"

"No, what?"

"Don't play coy with me, *RoughRider*."

"Say it." His tone is husky with desire. "Ask, and ye shall receive, my love."

"Fuck. Screw. Make love. Several times. In many positions."

He inhales sharply. "Hell yes."

"Thank God. When?"

"When did you say you're getting back?"

I try to calculate quickly. "I just need a few more days. Three, I think."

"So instead of going out the night you get home, how about if we stay in?"

"Yes. I want that more than anything."

"Me too."

I sigh heavily. "I have to get back to the office."

"See you soon, babe. Love you."

"I love you too."

I hear the slightest groan from him. "Say it one more time."

"RoughRider, I'm completely in love with you."

TWENTY-SEVEN

#sweetandsexy

I NEED TO see Jack first. As soon as my flight lands at O'Hare, I buy him some candy and a stuffed frog from the gift shop, then I race to the baggage claim, grab my bags, and locate my driver.

Eager as I am to get to Ryan—and I am *very* eager—I have to get in some time with Jack before that. Even though we've been Skyping, it's not the same. I need to lay eyes on him. Run my hand over his soft hair. Hear his voice and reassure myself that, for now, the little boy I know and love is still there.

As soon as the driver pulls up outside my brownstone, he offers to bring my bags inside. I slip him a bill, thank him, and hurry inside.

When I walk in the front door, instead of Carmen sitting on the couch, another woman is there.

"You must be Sienna," she says, standing up and offering me a hand. "I'm Lydia, one of the home health nurses."

"Oh, hi." I shake her hand, my gaze wandering over to the stairway. "How is he?"

"Good." She smiles, and I immediately like her. "He's having a few mental slips, but overall, he's doing just fine. Carmen is helping him with his bath now."

"Thanks. I'm going to run up and say hi."

As I climb the stairs, the sound of Jack and Carmen laughing brings tears to my eyes.

"Help me, Jack," she says, imitating a deep male voice. "Get me out of here."

"I'll save you, Han." Jack giggles.

I stop outside the door, the relief I feel making my shoulders slump forward. Right now, he's okay. It's a moment of joy.

"Sienna, is that you?" Jack calls.

"Yeah, I'm home. I missed you guys."

"You can come in," Carmen says. "Jack's up to his elbows in bubbles."

I round the corner and walk into the bathroom. Carmen is sitting on the edge of the tub, plastic *Star Wars* figurines lined up next to her.

"Look!" Jack pulls what looks like a giant ice cube out of the bubbles.

"What's that?" I step closer and see there's something inside the round ice chunk.

"Han Solo! We froze him in a cup of ice. Now I have to save him."

I smile. "Ah. Genius."

"Will you read me a bedtime story?"

"Of course I will. How about a *Pete the Cat* one?"

His eyes light up. "Yeah."

"Which one?"

He considers, his brow furrowed with confusion. "I don't know."

I exchange a brief look with Carmen. Jack always knows what story he wants. This is a reminder that we have a new normal now.

"How about if I surprise you?"

Jack nods enthusiastically, and Carmen gives me a grateful smile. I do the quick Carmen well-being check I've gotten good at now. Face—tired, but not as bad as it sometimes is. Clothes—rumpled, but not stained. Hair—clean.

She's okay. Okay as she can be, anyway.

I meet Jack in his bedroom, where I soak in the clean, soapy smell of him as he snuggles against me while I read him three books about his favorite blue cat.

"Are you leaving again?" he asks after the last book, his eyelids drooping with sleepiness.

"No. No trips for a while. I'm going to see Ryan tonight, but I'll be here when you wake up in the morning."

"Good." He yawns, and I tuck the covers around him. "Did you know we have nurses here now?"

"Yes. How do you like them?"

"They're nice."

"I'm glad." I smooth the damp hair on his forehead aside and kiss him. "Goodnight, sweet boy. I have presents for you tomorrow."

His eyes widen, and he grins. "Presents? Did you bring me an apple?"

"No, silly. Why would I do that?"

"Because you were in the Big Apple."

I laugh and reach down to hug him. There's something to be said for treasuring every hug. Every laugh. Every good day. Most of us don't know how long we'll have in this life, but with Jack, we know. His whole life will be lived as a sweet, innocent little boy. I wish he could understand that loving him has changed me forever.

"Goodnight, Jack," I whisper, smoothing the hair back from his forehead again.

"Night, Cici."

AN HOUR LATER, I'm on Ryan's doorstep, showered and dressed in jeans and a long-sleeved black T-shirt. I decided not to toil over my outfit, since it will be on the floor shortly after I walk into Ryan's home.

He lives in a modest, neat, nearly new duplex. I take a deep breath and knock on the steel front door. As soon as Ryan opens it, I fly into his arms.

I barely even got a look at him, but I saw a navy T-shirt and gray shorts. What matters more in this moment is how he feels. He's warm and solid, our chests pressed together as I bury my face in his neck and take in his freshly showered scent.

"I missed you," he says in a low tone, his breath on my ear sending a shiver of awareness through me.

He lifts me up and gently closes the front door with his foot. My arms are wrapped around his back, and I hold on with everything I've got.

"You okay?" he asks.

"Yeah." My voice is muffled against his neck.

I relax my grip and let my feet slide down to the floor. When I look up at him, his dark eyes are swirling with soft affection and hot intensity at the same time.

"I was thinking on my flight about how lucky we are to be together," I say, reaching up to cup his scruffy cheek. "If I hadn't done that interview, and if you hadn't seen it . . . and if Isabella Moore hadn't shown up in my office that day while I happened to be chatting with you . . . none of this would be happening."

"I was haunted by what-ifs for years." Ryan gently grips my hips with his big hands. "What if you found someone and got married was the worst one."

"Love is actually pretty terrifying, isn't it?" My lips are so close to his I can feel the warmth of his mouth.

He groans softly and slides a hand up, cupping the back of my neck. "It's kind of like jumping off a cliff while blindfolded." He brushes his lips over mine. "But it's also exhilarating." Another soft kiss. "All-encompassing." A long, lingering kiss that makes my heart race. "And completely worth taking a leap for."

When his hand sinks into my ass in a possessive hold, I moan and slide a hand down his chest.

"I'd jump off a thousand cliffs for you, Sienna," Ryan says, resting his forehead against mine. "You're everything to me."

"Show me." I step out of his arms and pull my shirt up and off over my head, dropping it on the floor.

Ryan's gaze darkens as it roams my body, and I feel like a goddess. I never knew it was possible to feel so punch-drunk on someone's reactions to me. As I slide out of my jeans, his eyes can't seem to keep up. He's looking at every inch of me, his breathing getting faster.

"In the bedroom," he murmurs, taking my hand to lead the way.

He strips off his T-shirt and slides down his shorts as I lie back on the bed. Every nerve ending in my body is on alert, buzzing with hot awareness. When Ryan climbs on top of me, instinct takes over.

I don't have to think anymore. I just *feel*, completely overwhelmed by the sensations. His stubble brushes across every inch of my skin as he delivers on his earlier promise, slowly touching each and every inch of me.

It's not like it's been with other men. With Ryan, I don't worry about pretense. I don't feel self-conscious. When I need to, I take one of his hands and slide it across my stomach and down between my legs, eliciting a groan from him.

There's nothing I won't give Ryan, and there's nothing I won't take. I want it all. When he finally unfastens my bra and cups my breasts in his hands, our mingled moans fill the room.

I realize with sudden clarity what people mean when they say love is a verb. We've spoken the words, but here in this room right now, Ryan and I are loving each other as an action. I've never felt more adored than I do right now, and I've never wanted to satisfy a man so completely.

He slips my panties off, then takes off his own boxer briefs and rolls a condom over his long, hard shaft. His eyes are on mine as he slides inside me, and I cry out from the wave of pleasure I feel.

It's never, ever been like this before. I wrap my arms around Ryan's waist as we move together, lost in each other. With every thrust that fills me, I'm complete. And every time he moves back, I crave that fullness like my lungs crave air.

My fingertips dig into his back, and my legs hold tight to his hips as I come, whimpering his name as a tear slips out of the corner of one eye. I grind against him, riding out every wave that washes over me.

He kisses me then, a slight smile dancing on his lips. And then, he fills me again, this time with a hard intensity that makes me swear and immediately beg for more.

It's hot and fast this time, and when he hooks a hand behind one of my legs and sinks in just a bit farther, I bite down on his neck, and he groans his approval.

I've never loved a man until now, I realize as we approach the brink together. This is that magical, all-in love I'd pretty much given up on. It's not something I could explain to anyone, but something I feel soul-deep. Ryan is my one and only.

The muscles in his neck and shoulders stand out as he holds on to his orgasm, keeping it leashed like a beast desperate for release. When I start to come, he groans with the effort of keeping control, and then, finally, he cedes to the demand, his entire body shuddering with release.

We're quiet for a couple minutes, just breathing hard and holding on to each other.

"Worth the wait?" I murmur against his sweaty chest.

He exhales a note of laughter. "More than worth it. I hope you know you're stuck with me now. I can never even look at another woman after that."

"I was kind of hoping to be stuck with you for a really long time." I kiss his chest and lean up on an elbow, smiling down at him.

He rubs a lock of my hair between his thumb and forefinger, affection swimming in his gaze. "Forever is a long time," he says softly. "And yet, not long enough."

"I love you, Ryan. More than I can even say. I love you more than Starbucks."

He gives me the playful grin that makes my pulse pound. "High praise, babe. More than Oreos?"

"So much more than Oreos. I'd give up Oreos for you." I pretend to consider. "I mean, all but the double-stuffed ones."

In a flash, he flips me onto my back and leans over me, his gaze hungry once again. "I'll double stuff *you*, baby."

I laugh and run my foot up the inside of his leg. "Big talk, RoughRider. I thought you were a man of action."

With a soft groan, he arches his brows and says, "Valid point. I'll show you. And you haven't even seen rough yet, by the way."

Hell. Yes.

He's right—forever isn't long enough. But I'll treasure every moment I get with him, and never stop appreciating the joy we've found in each other.

EPILOGUE

One Month Later

RYAN WRAPS ME up in a hug that sweeps me off my feet. He swings me around, smiling as I grab his cheeks and kiss him.

"You know how I feel about undefeated football coaches," I murmur against his lips.

A satisfied rumble sounds in his throat. "Counting on it, babe."

After a close home game, his team just held on to its undefeated record. Since he's the coach, I know Ryan is thrilled for his team, but he's also got to be looking forward to our post-game celebration.

After every win, he scores. Usually several times. Often in the shower before he even makes it to bed. There's something about the sight of his back on the sidelines during games, his broad shoulders and firm, round ass on display, that gets me going.

When Ryan sets me down, I see a blue flash out of the corner of my eye as Coop flies by with Jack on his shoulders. Jack's giggle makes me smile, as always.

At every Oakhurst home game, Jack is now the official Gatorade keeper. He sits next to a giant cooler, opening it and handing out Gatorades to players who want one. When Ryan gave him the job, he lit up like a Christmas tree. Carmen never thought Jack would be part of a sports team in any way, and she still tears up as we sit in the bleachers and watch him proudly doing his job. The players ask him to do other jobs for them, like test out the field before games and hold the ball. I don't know if they realize how much it means to him, but I've considered offering all of them college scholarships and internships because of how much it means to me.

Ryan wraps an arm around my shoulders and kisses my temple. "I have to go, babe."

I lean in and give him a quick kiss. "Hey, should we take the coaching staff out for pizza?"

"Sure, sounds good. We can't stay super late, though." He arches a brow.

"Don't worry. I'm as eager as you are."

When he kisses me again, some of his players hoot and holler at us. We don't mind. Those boys should be so lucky to find what we've got.

Coop takes Jack, still on his shoulders, over to where the players are, and they line up, each one giving Jack a high five on their way into the locker room.

"Can I take him in?" Coop asks Carmen, smiling sheepishly.

"Into the locker room?"

"Yes!" Jack answers for her, bouncing with excitement.

"Sure." Carmen's eyes soften with gratitude toward Coop.

We watch them leave, and Carmen's wistful expression matches my mood.

"Your brother's pretty great, Sienna," she says.

"He is."

She turns my way and grins. "And your boyfriend's not so bad either."

My smile widens. "I can't freakin' believe I have a boyfriend."

"I love seeing you so happy. You deserve it."

"You deserve it too."

She shrugs. "I've got all I need right now."

I hum my skepticism. "I caught you looking at my brother like a gallon of ice water in a desert earlier."

She flushes. "Leave me alone, I'm only human."

"Why don't you let me and Ryan take Jack somewhere next time Coop has a day off and the two of you can . . . hang out?"

"Hang out, huh?"

I put up a hand to stop her. "No further details. Ever. He's my brother."

She smiles. "Maybe."

We sit down on the bench the players vacated.

"Funny how hope and happiness can be harder than just expecting the worst," Carmen says. "It's so easy to assume nothing will ever work out."

"I built a business on that assumption," I remind her. "But I was wrong." I wrap an arm around her, the brisk fall wind feeling chilly now. "And being wrong has never felt so good."

BRENDA ROTHERT LIVES in Central Illinois. She was a daily print journalist for nine years, during which time she enjoyed writing a wide range of stories.

These days Brenda writes Contemporary Romance. She loves to hear from readers.

CONNECT WITH BRENDA

www.brendarothert.com

Dirty Work (with Chelle Bliss)

Dirty Secret (with Chelle Bliss)

His

Hooked

Come Closer

Protecting Sarina (Kindle Worlds Novella)

ACKNOWLEDGEMENTS

EVERY BOOK I write takes me outside of myself emotionally. To write the thoughts and feelings of my characters, I have to get inside their heads and take myself to the places they are. And for Alpha Mail, I had to write about the slow, painful loss of a beloved child.

I had the framework of the story outlined going in, and it was important to me that Jack have an illness he couldn't recover from. I want to represent real people and their lives in my books, and there are families out there facing Batten's disease and other serious childhood illnesses.

Outlining the details is one thing. Going there emotionally was quite another. I'm a mom, and there's nothing I'm more thankful for than my healthy children. To anyone out there caring for a seriously ill child, God Bless You. May you continue to find the strength you need. I used to say, "I can't imagine," but now, I have imagined, and it's a dark, terribly sad place to go.

There are several different kinds of love in this story. Not just Ryan and Sienna's, but also Carmen and Sienna's, Jack and Carmen's, Jack and Sienna's and Coop and Sienna's. Those different kinds of love lifted me up as I wrote this. Love isn't one-size-fits-all, and we all need different kinds of love, not just the romantic sort.

I truly couldn't have written this book without the help of my incredible production team. With every book, they pull me through the hard times and celebrate the end, even though it's inevitably late and leaves them scrambling to do their parts. My author bestie Stephanie Reid came through with her usual plotting magic. I can't say enough thank yous to beta readers Chelle Northcutt,

Janett Gomez, Chantal Gemperle, and Michelle Tan, line editor Lisa Hollett (who edited most of this book while traveling and still rocked it), copy editor Taylor Bellitto, and interior designer/formatter Christine Borgford. These women partner with me to bring you everything you find between the covers of my books. I treasure every one of them.

The talents of Photographer Sara Eirew and Cover Designer Regina Wamba combined into a cover I'm incredibly proud of. My publicist Jessica Estep was with me every step of the way on this book, cheering me on, listening to me when I was down and getting me motivated with her amazing promo ideas. She is part publicist, part friend, and wholly amazing.

My friend J inspired a chapter of this book. I'm grateful he cares enough to be engaged in my work and throw out ideas when I need them.

Hat tips to my assistant Pam Million and my friend Pam Carrion for always being there. They keep things moving when I'm in the cave, and it means everything.

Biggest thanks of all to every reader who continues to take a chance on my work. I couldn't do this without you.

www.ingramcontent.com/pod-product-compliance
Lightning Source LLC
Chambersburg PA
CBHW060211180626
46813CB00007B/2783